Lesia's Dream

LESIA'S DREAM

Laura Langston

 HarperTrophyCanada®

An imprint of HarperCollins*Publishers*Ltd

Lesia's Dream

This is a work of historical fiction, and any resemblance to people either living or dead is purely coincidental.

First edition

HarperCollins books may be purchased for educational, business, or sales promotional use through our Special Markets Department.

HarperCollins Publishers Ltd.
2 Bloor Street East, 20th Floor
Toronto, Ontario, Canada
M4W 1A8

www.harpercanada.com

National Library of Canada Cataloguing in Publication

Langston, Laura
Lesia's dream / Laura Langston.

ISBN 0-00-639283-0

1. Ukrainians – Canada – Juvenile fiction. I. Title.

PS8573.A5832L48 2003 jC813'.54
C2003-903014-8
PZ7

HC 9 8 7 6 5 4 3 2 1

Printed and bound in the United States
Set in Bembo

FOR MY MOTHER-IN-LAW,
MARY NAZARKO,
WITH LOVE

We are not born all at once, but by bits.
The body first, and the spirit later.

—Mary Antin,
The Promised Land

Prologue

January 2003

Winnipeg, Manitoba

You come to me young and fresh, full of questions. I sit here, old and weary, full of memories. In that school with all its rooms and teachers and so many pencils that you have no need to share, they have asked you to speak of your roots. Something called your heritage. You are Canadian, you tell them. Born here. Just as your mother and grandmother were born here.

Before, they say. Before.

You do not know of heritage. You know only of me.

You are so tall, though you are only sixteen. At sixteen, my face showed hard lines of worry and my hair, once long and beautiful, had become dull and brittle. But your face is unlined, full of promise. Your hair has the rich, golden shine of the honey we gathered in Shuparka. Your world is different from the one I lived in at sixteen.

Other babas are sad about this. Some are even mad. But I accept. Because accepting brings me peace.

You are not of the old world. You are firmly of the new. But you are tied to me. Oh, yes. Tied to me forever.

Laisha.

They told me you were named for me. I told them your name is not my name. It is not true to custom.

But now . . . now I think your name is beautiful. It is all that is good from me and my time, sprung forth into all that is new and wonderful in your time.

It is the freedom I dreamed of when I was your age.

Ach, sixteen. Back then, I carried within me the egg that would become your grandmother, the egg that would become your mother and the one that would become you. Yes, I carried generations in my loins. And even then I carried memories.

I carried the spring smell of the fruit blossoms in Shuparka. The sound of the wind whistling through the beekeeper's hut. The feel of Baba's arms around me as we said goodbye. That first glimpse of the prairie. Especially that.

The prairie changed me. Just as I changed it.

I am old. My eyes are failing. My legs are weak. But my memories are strong. And they have been silent for too long.

Pull up a chair and listen, for soon my body shall disappear from this earth. Traces of me will remain, oh, yes. In the prairie I cleared, the wheat I planted, the family I buried. In brown eyes that are thickly lashed and far seeing. In strong, sure hands that are meant for working the soil, for turning the pyrohy dough. You have them both, dear Laisha. Just as your daughter shall have them and, so too, the daughter that follows her.

I will answer your questions about roots and heritage. And that will satisfy them. But it will not satisfy me. Heritage is like soil. And soil is nothing without seeds. So I give you these memories as seeds. I hope you will honour them and cherish them and pass them along so they may grow and ripen and nourish you, your daughter and her daughters forever.

Chapter One

March 1914

Shuparka
Province of Galicia
Austro-Hungarian Empire

Lesia's day had started before dawn. Turning the landowner's wet, spring soil had been hard, heavy work. Though her thin arms were strong, after twelve hours of lifting they ached with fatigue. But though the gnawing hunger in her belly usually made her light-headed and grumpy, it didn't today. Today Master Stryk had paid her well and given her a large bundle of wood besides.

She could hide another rynsky!

Clutching the bundle of wood under her arm, she pulled up her skirt and ran through the village. Coins tumbled happily in her pocket. The setting sun cast a golden glow over the thatched roofs of the nearby houses. In a few weeks, the spring air would be filled with the rich, sweet scent of plum blossoms flowering near the beekeeper's hut in the grove.

Lesia was so hungry she could taste the plums now. Stewed with honey and linden flowers. And in babka at Easter, if they were lucky enough to have flour by then.

The fence that had once surrounded their small cottage was gone, burned long ago to keep them warm, but the gate still stood on its posts, swaying in the breeze as it often did. Lesia nudged it shut with her foot, raced down the dirt path, pushed open the thick, wooden door and hurried inside.

"Mama, Baba, come quick."

Mama was nowhere to be found, but Baba was low on her heels, poking at a pot over the fire. "What is it, child?" The old woman stood up and frowned. The skin of her face collapsed into prune-like folds. "What's wrong?"

Lesia giggled. "Nothing's *wrong*!" She shoved the bundle of wood at her grandmother. "Here." She reached into her pocket. "And here." She held out seven rynskys. The eighth stayed in her apron. Guilt tugged at her conscience. She knew what she was doing was right, but it still *felt* wrong.

"Bozhe! Bozhe! A bundle of wood *and* seven rynskys." Baba's smile slipped. She squinted suspiciously. "How come they give you so much?" Baba had been furious four years ago when Lesia had turned eleven and had gone to work in the landowner's fields. Serfdom was over, her grandmother had said angrily. Lesia should go to school. But there was no school in the village. Besides, earning money for wood and food was more important than an education.

Lesia grabbed the old woman's hands. The wood tumbled to the floor. "Because I work hard, so very hard." Grinning broadly, she swung her grandmother back and forth. "And tomorrow they have asked me to assist with the bees." That was her favourite thing to do.

She stopped mid-step. Something smelled wonderful, and it was more than the potatoes they'd been living on for weeks. "I must be dreaming," she said slowly. "I smell bread."

"There." The old lady pointed to a crusty loaf cooling in the corner.

When Lesia's eyes widened, Baba patted her cheek. "Ivan and Papa are home. They brought flour."

Lesia's heart jumped. "Where are they?"

"Out back." Baba started to cough.

Lesia flung herself out the back door. "Papa! Ivan!"

There was Papa, wearing the same black pants he'd worn nine months ago when he'd left home to search for work. His moustache was greyer and his eyes were tired, but he offered her the same crooked smile, the same open arms.

"Lesia!" His whiskers tickled her cheek as he kissed her. "I've missed you, moye sonechko."

My sunshine. Oh, how she'd yearned to hear that phrase! "And I've missed you too, Papa." His sheepskin coat smelled faintly of tobacco; it was smooth and cool against her face.

"Well, sister, I hope you've taken good care of the bees while I was away."

"Ivan!" She swung around to greet her brother. He hadn't returned for Christmas like Papa, and Lesia had missed him. He was standing near the bee skep. It had been golden brown when he'd left, the colour of flax before it flowered. Now, it had weathered to a soft dove grey.

Lesia stared. Ivan was older, thinner. With his new clothes

and moustache, he looked more like Papa than ever. "You look so different."

"It's been three-quarters of a year. I'm an old man of seventeen now, you know." He shuffled his feet and pretended to walk with a cane.

They all laughed, even little Sonia, who clapped her hands and excitedly bobbed her head up and down, up and down.

"Did you find it?" Lesia demanded. "The big money we talked about?"

"Lesia!" her mother chided. Sonia was squirming and clapping. Mama put her down. "That's silly talk."

But Mama didn't know about Lesia and Ivan's plan. They'd told no one. Not even Baba. "Did you?" she demanded again.

Ivan's eyes gleamed with excitement. He nodded. "We're almost there, Lesia. How about you? Did you manage to save?"

"A little." She nodded. "Twenty-four rynskys so far. After today, twenty-five."

Papa looked at Mama. Mama looked at Papa. They both looked confused. "What are you two talking about?" Papa asked.

She grinned at Ivan. "You tell them!"

"Lesia and I are going to Canada," Ivan said. "We want you to come with us."

"Canada!" Mama looked shocked. "That's halfway around the world. We cannot afford to—"

Ivan interrupted her. "We've been working and saving, Mama. We have over six hundred rynskys."

Lesia smothered a gasp. Ivan had obviously done well in his travels.

Mama clutched her throat and turned the colour of an eggshell. Papa's eyes widened in disbelief. "Six hundred rynskys?" he repeated.

"Yes!" Ivan said triumphantly. "Just a little more and we'll be ready to leave for Canada."

"We are not going anywhere." Papa repeated the words he'd said so many times before. "The Magus family belongs in Ukraine just as the great Dnister crests its banks in spring. I will not give up on this land."

Lesia's stomach flipped nervously. Her grin faded. "We have nothing here, Papa. In Canada we'll have wood and land and food. We'll be rich beyond belief!"

Wordlessly, Papa shook his head. She'd been so sure he would change his mind once the money was saved. Dejected, her stomach sank to her toes.

Mama looked sad. "You dream, my darling Lesia. You think you'll be a tsarivna and live in a grand palace too one day."

"That's not it at all!" Impatiently, Lesia brushed away a fly. "How much heartache must we suffer? How many more deaths must we witness?" She couldn't stop the words. "Think how different our lives would be if we'd gone five years ago!"

Mama gasped. If they'd left back then, Slavko would still be alive. Maybe even her beloved Geedo. "Nothing can be done to change things," she murmured. "As God ordains, so it shall be."

Lesia stared at the ground. It was Mama's usual response.

"We've talked about this." Papa rubbed his moustache wearily. "More than half the village has given up and left, and look at what we hear back. Some say Canada is the land of milk and honey. Others say it's the frozen land of Hell. We don't know who to believe."

"We are visitors in our own land," Ivan said grimly. "First the Russians oppressed us, now it's the Austrians and the Poles. Slavery ended over fifty years ago, but we're not really free. They've taken away our right to have a Ukrainian nation. They won't even let us call ourselves Ukrainians. We have to call ourselves Ruthenians instead." With a twist of his lips, he stared beyond the small patch of black soil Baba had prepared for planting, beyond the cherished bee skep, to the house on the rise where the landowner lived.

Ivan turned back to Mama and Papa. "Most of our land has been taken, and we're being taxed to death. We have no wood for fuel and almost nowhere to grow food. We're practically starving." He paused and looked at Lesia. They were both thinking the same thing. Slavko. And Geedo. "It's time to get out!"

"It's those people you associate with," Papa muttered. "Teaching you to read and write. Putting strange ideas in your head." Mama was close to tears. "Look at the trouble you caused handing out books, holding meetings and encouraging Ukrainians to join together against the state." Papa's voice slipped to a whisper. "You take great risks, Ivan."

It was true. Ivan did take risks. And Master Stryk had been livid when he'd learned of Ivan's activities. But then Slavko had died, and everything had changed. After that, Ivan had become more careful, secretive almost. And he and Lesia had made a vow. They would do whatever it took to get out of Ukraine.

"You know the law," Lesia said. "Ivan will be eighteen soon. They force all Ukrainian males to join the army. He'll never be able to leave then. We must get out while we can!"

Mama and Papa were silent.

"You are right about one thing, Papa. This is our soil." Ivan stomped his foot against the earth and a small puff of dirt rose into the air. "And I would lay down my life for it. But there is going to be a war. I won't be able to fight for Ukraine. I'll be caught between two enemies, fighting for the Austrians or the Poles. Maybe even the Russians, if they invade." His eyes darkened. "No matter whose side we're on, they'll take what little land we have left. Our only hope is Canada. Their door is wide open. If we don't go now, we'll never have another chance."

Sonia was toddling between Lesia's legs. She lurched back and forth and then, with a thump, she fell backwards onto the ground, letting out a wail. Lesia picked her up.

"War?" Mama looked at Papa.

Papa stared into the distance, beyond the house on the rise, to where the sun was setting in streaks of golden pink.

Lesia waited. Ivan told the truth.

"War is possible," Papa finally admitted. "I've thought about that too. Leaving is a risk. But with another child coming and only three morgens of land to split among all of you, staying is also risky. Yet Master Stryk is a kind man."

"He may be kind," Ivan agreed, "but if there is a war, he will be helpless."

Lesia wasn't interested in Master Stryk. "Another baby?" She jiggled Sonia on her hip. It seemed like only yesterday her younger sister had arrived!

Mama patted her stomach. "By fall," she said softly.

No wonder Mama hadn't made it up the hill to work the last few days. Lesia remembered how tired Mama was carrying Sonia.

"We have just three morgens of land here." Ivan was still talking to Papa. "Remember what the land agents said. In Canada, the government provides immigrants with 113 morgens, 160 acres!" He shook his head from side to side in awe. "And it's almost free for the taking."

"Not free," Papa said cautiously. "And travel is expensive."

"We'll need close to eight hundred rynskys, which is about three hundred Canadian dollars," Ivan said in a rush, "but we're almost there, Papa."

Papa was silent. Then he said, "Someone told me Canada expects immigrants to bring in a little extra money. Insurance money almost, so they aren't a burden while they get established."

Mama looked stunned. Lesia couldn't contain her grin. Papa was changing his mind!

"We'll have to sell our holdings to Master Stryk." Ivan looked triumphant. "Raise more money. Perhaps borrow some."

Papa frowned. "I will not go into debt."

"I cannot believe you would give up on Ukraine." Mama's eyes shimmered with tears. She turned to stare at the small white cross that marked Slavko's grave. "My heart tells me to stay. And decisions of the heart are never wrong."

Lesia swallowed the lump in her throat. Her younger brother had died two years ago at the age of eleven. He'd been too hungry and too weak to resist the virus that had swept through the village. Geedo had died the year before. Baba still grieved for her husband. "We cannot live in the past, Mama. We must go forward. It's the only way we'll survive."

"Lesia and Ivan are going to Canada," Papa said firmly. "We

belong together. And Lesia's right. We must go forward. It's time for change."

Finally, what she and Ivan had dreamed was coming true! "We aren't giving up, Mama," Lesia said. "We'll make a new home for ourselves in Canada. We'll live rich. We'll live free!"

Mama looked doubtful. Gently, Papa reassured her. "There will be time to get used to the idea, Ahafia. It will be many months before we have enough money to travel."

Lesia and Ivan exchanged glances. Papa was wrong.

Chapter Two

It was dark when Lesia rose from the narrow bed she shared with Sonia. Tiptoeing past Ivan and Baba, she let herself outside and raced up the hill. She and Ivan had talked late into the night, and they had both reached the same uneasy conclusion. If Lesia didn't succeed at their plan, Canada would be lost forever.

Though it was early, the older villagers were already trickling into the landowner's manor. As one of the younger servants, Lesia was supposed to wait outside in the cold for her list of chores. But today she moved swiftly through the kitchen, making sure to hide from Kasia, the kitchen boss, who liked to lord it over the poor peasants. Lucky for her, the heavy-set woman was barking out orders and didn't see Lesia slip past.

Down the hall she went, stopping at the landowner's ornate

wooden door. It was closed. Jan Stryk was an early riser, and he often put in several hours of work before breakfast. She hoped he was at his desk today.

She raised her fist and knocked.

"Yes?"

Answering would have been the proper thing to do, but there was nothing proper about any of this. Instead she turned the handle, pushed the door open and walked bravely into his study.

Master Stryk was bent over his red ledger book. A small lamp with a white shade cast thin shadows onto the wall behind him. "Yes?" he repeated impatiently, continuing to write.

Lesia's heart raced. Papa would be furious if he knew what she was about to ask. But if Master Stryk said yes, there would be little Papa could do.

Jan Stryk looked up. His rheumy old eyes softened. "Lesia Magus." A smile crept across his wrinkled face. "Come in."

She bowed low in front of him. "Glory to God." Her voice trembled as she said the familiar, comforting words. She reached for his leathery hand and kissed it.

"What can I do for you, child?" Jan Stryk's chair squeaked as he leaned back and studied her. Other members of the Polish nobility ruled through harshness and intimidation. Not Master Stryk. His very kindness was one of the reasons her father had insisted they stay behind in Shuparka. And the landowner's generosity was legend.

"Sir, I . . . we . . . my family . . . we have decided to follow the others and go to Canada." She licked her dry lips.

"You're tired of working my land?"

She started to shake her head but stopped. She *was* tired of working his land. She wanted to work her own. "In Canada, there's plenty of land to go around," she said. "There's wood . . . and plenty of food."

"So I've heard."

He wasn't making this easy for her. "I . . . we—"

"Let me guess," Master Stryk said dryly, "you want me to buy your three morgens of land."

"No. I mean, yes. But that's something Papa will have to discuss with you."

Master Stryk looked confused. "Then why are you here?"

She took a deep breath. "Selling our land won't give us enough money to go."

A ghost of a smile flitted across the old man's face. "Why hasn't your father approached me about this?"

"My father is a cautious man. He doesn't like loans."

"Does he know you're here?"

"No." Heat prickled her cheeks. "This isn't something I ask easily or lightly," she said in a rush. "We have some money. But not enough for all of us."

"How much more do you need?"

"One hundred rynskys." Her voice trembled.

"Ah," Master Stryk said again. He leaned forward. "What guarantee do I have that you'll pay me back?"

"You have my word. My honour! And my father's honour," Lesia vowed. "We will send money each month. We will work hard to pay you back."

"You're a hard worker. So is your father." He tapped two fingers thoughtfully against his blotter as he studied Lesia. "I hear he has returned, and Ivan too." He raised an eyebrow.

"I certainly would like to see your brother take his politics and leave this village for good." He opened a drawer and began shuffling through papers. "Where would you settle?"

Hope flared. Master Stryk wasn't just making polite conversation! Was he? Perhaps. Hope died again. "The Interlake, sir. That's where the Czumers settled."

"Ah yes. Your young friend Mary Czumer. I miss her wonderful laugh." The old man's head was bent. He was still searching. "Here we are." He removed a small black book and reached for a pen. Slowly he began to write.

What was he doing? Lesia wondered. According to village gossip, Master Stryk had a small tin money box hidden in his desk. She had prayed he would reach in, remove one hundred rynskys and give them to her. Instead he was giving her a piece of paper. A piece of paper was worthless. She couldn't even read it.

"Here," he said, "take this paper to the—"

There were two impatient raps on the door. Michal Stryk strode into the room. "Father, breakfast is ready. I've come to collect you." He stared down his long nose at Lesia. "What are you doing here?" He planted a hand on either side of his large belly and rocked back onto his heels. "Shouldn't you have your head in a beehive somewhere?" His lips thinned into a smirk.

"I'll be with you in a moment, Michal." The older man ignored his son's rudeness and handed Lesia a small square of cream-coloured paper. "Take this to the bank and they will give you one hundred rynskys. I expect you to pay me back, of course. As time permits."

Bozhe! He had said yes. "Thank you, sir. We *will* pay you

back. Quickly too." She leaned forward and took the small slip of paper from his gnarled fingers.

Michal snatched it away from her. "Father!" Horrified, he waved the paper in the air. "How much more of our money are you going to give away?"

Her heart thudded. She stared from son to father.

"Give it back to her, Michal," Master Stryk ordered.

"You can't be serious!" Michal's face flushed with anger, a stain that rose from under the collar of his shirt. "Look at her. She is a dirty, uneducated peasant. Why are you giving her money?"

A dirty peasant? She was proud of her peasant ancestry!

"I am not giving her money," Master Stryk replied. "I am lending it to her. So she may go to Canada."

"Canada!" Michal Stryk snorted. "Her? She is so thin and frail, she won't make it to Canada. She is all eyes and elbows. She has no substance. She is a weakling, just like the rest of that Magus family. She can barely cultivate the flax and tend the bees." His face went redder and redder until it was the colour of a bowl of borsch. "She and that brother of hers would wipe us Poles off the face of the map if they could. All for some pathetic Ukraine." He spat the last word out through narrowed lips.

Pathetic Ukraine? No substance? How dare he?

Master Stryk looked at Lesia. "You must excuse my son. His manners are less than exemplary." He turned back to Michal. "Give her back the paper," he ordered a second time.

Michal stared at his father. "All right," he said slowly. "I will give it to her. If she can read it, she can keep it." He handed the small piece of paper to Lesia. "Well?" he challenged with a sneer.

The prickling in her cheeks spread to her forehead, her ears, the back of her neck. She didn't look at the paper. There was no point. Instead she stared defiantly at Michal Stryk. "I don't read."

He hooted. "You see, Father? She is useless. Stupid. Brainless. It's shameful giving a worthless servant like this your money. Giving her *my* inheritance!"

Useless. Stupid. Brainless. She stared at a narrow crack between the floorboards. She wanted to shrink until she could hide there. Never in her entire life had she felt so humiliated.

Master Stryk glared at his son. "When I am dead and gone, you will make the decisions. While I am alive, I make them. I am still in charge here, Michal. I pay the bills and I issue the pay. Including, it seems to me, yours."

"But she is a peasant," Michal argued hotly. "You cannot trust her to pay you back. We will never see that money again!"

Lesia opened her mouth to speak but thought better of it. How dare he even suggest such a thing? She was trustworthy!

The old man's eyebrows stretched into one long frown. "I will take my chances."

"You are foolish, Father. Giving away our money. Allowing the peasants to emigrate." Michal flung open the door. "Soon the rynskys will be gone. And there will be no one left to work the land." He slammed the door behind him.

The sound made her jump. Her heart thumped nervously. She pressed a hand to her chest.

"He is young and foolish," Master Stryk said with an embarrassed smile. "He does not mean what he says."

The master was simply trying to make her feel better.

Michal Stryk meant exactly what he said. Lesia had lived with cruelty and disdain from the aristocracy all her life. She had shivered through many cold nights and gone hungry for many winters because of it. Papa said it was all a political misunderstanding that would eventually straighten itself out. Ivan said they needed to fight for their rights. Suddenly, Lesia realized that Papa and Ivan were both wrong.

The truth was simple but shattering. She was not valued as a human being. As a Ukrainian peasant, she was considered worthless, brainless, useless. Michal's words scorched her soul. Praise to God that she was getting out while she could! And going to a place where she would be respected, where her skills as a steward of the land, a fledgling beekeeper, would be valued.

"I'm sorry," Master Stryk said softly.

"Your son is wrong about one thing." She was amazed that her voice was so *normal!* "We shall repay you. I give you my word of honour. We will send you money from Canada. A little each month, until our debt is cleared."

Master Stryk looked across the desk. Sadness, defeat and admiration flickered in his eyes. He smiled softly. "Go, quickly, child. Remember, you may always return. There will always be work for you in my house. God be with you."

* * *

Five weeks later, most of the village came to say goodbye. Warm bodies and laughing chatter filled the small cottage as Lesia slipped outside and hurried down the path to the horse and wagon.

They were leaving for Hamburg in less than an hour, and she was terrified that they had forgotten something. She wanted to check the trunk one last time.

The air was cool and her fingers stiff as she fumbled with the large, round lock on the sturdy brown trunk Papa had built. It was impossible to believe that everything precious was inside! Her family's entire life reduced to one brown box. Strange.

On the bottom were winter clothes, bedsheets and two quilts. Next came an axe, a handsaw and a hammer for building, a spade, a sickle, a hoe and the leathers of a flail for working the land. Baba's one and only kylym, her tapestry, was tucked firmly between pillows. And Mama and Baba had still found room to slip in their precious ikons: a picture of the Blessed Virgin, the cross painstakingly carved by Geedo years ago and a small bottle of holy water from the river Dnister. There were thirty bundles of garden seeds to plant when they arrived, folds of muslin stuffed with dried herbs to use for healing as well as onions, garlic and horseradish to both eat and plant. Ivan had demanded room for all his books, but in the end, he had been forced to reduce his selection to just two. When Papa had asked Lesia what she wanted to include, she had silently handed him a white handkerchief with a small scoop of soil from Slavko's grave. Their one and only sheepskin coat had been laid on top before the lid was pushed shut.

It was all there. All in its place. But it must have settled overnight because there was now more than an inch of room between the sheepskin and the top of the trunk. Strange how that worked.

Footsteps fell on the path behind her. "Darling, we must talk."

It was Baba. "Why aren't you inside saying goodbye to everyone?" Lesia asked.

"I'm staying behind," the old woman said. "I am too old to travel. Too set in my ways. But you must go to Canada and follow your dreams."

"Baba, no! We can't leave without you."

Baba touched Lesia's cheek. Her fingers were thick and coarse, lovingly familiar. "I will be fine. Like Papa said, Master Stryk is not so bad."

She wouldn't leave Baba behind. She *couldn't*. "I will stay with you until the others are settled. Until the house is built," Lesia decided suddenly, "and then you and I can join them."

"You must go. They will need you. But I cannot leave Geedo and Slavko. Besides, Shuparka is my home." The old woman coughed and her whole body shook.

"Baba, your cough. I cannot leave. Who will care for you?"

"Ach, it's just the cough of winter. It's clearing already, now that the weather has warmed." Clearing her throat, she pulled a crock from the folds of her apron. "This honey will feed you on your journey, but let it also feed your soul. Remember always the bees. Their work is their joy. They work long and they work hard, and always they work together, but ah, how sweet their reward. Let your effort be true, my darling child, and your rewards will be sweet."

"Baba, please!" She could feel her lower lip quivering. She didn't trust herself to speak. Darling, darling Baba. How could they leave her behind?

"Hush!" The old woman held one finger to her lips before pulling something else from her apron. "And you must take this with you too."

Geedo's Bible! The one where he had painstakingly recorded the family history as far back as he could remember. Lesia's fingers folded around the familiar worn leather. The Bible was one of Baba's most precious possessions. She couldn't read it herself, but it was her last link to the man she had married so many years ago.

The lump in Lesia's throat grew too big to ignore. "Oh, Baba!" Her voice cracked. Tears ran like salty rivers down her cheeks. The old woman folded her tight against her bosom and rocked her back and forth.

"I can't take the Bible, Baba," Lesia finally managed to say. "Not that."

Gently Baba pulled back. "And I cannot give you my heart, dear one. So I give you this." She touched her fingers to the worn leather and then touched her heart. "When you hold it close, you hold me close."

Lesia stared into the face that had always been there for her. Baba was the wisest. The one she depended on the most. "I can't go without you, Baba."

The old woman sighed and reached for her again. "Hold Geedo's Bible close and you hold me close. It will comfort you. It will help you keep the faith."

"But Michal Stryk was right, Baba. I cannot read. I am unworthy of this gift." *Useless. Stupid. Brainless.*

"Such silliness!" Baba smoothed her hair in a comforting gesture. "Do you think I would give Geedo's Bible to just anyone? Ach. No! I give the Bible to you because in God's eyes we are all worthy. We are all somebody. You are Lesia Magus, part of my heart. Part of Geedo's heart."

Lesia wiggled out of her arms. "But Baba—"

The old woman held up a finger. There was a fierce, determined look in her eyes. "There are many Michals in this world," she warned. "And they would like us to live beneath them. I have seen this too. But in the eyes of God, we are all equal. Peasants and landowners. Ukrainians and Canadians. The Bible will help you remember."

Lesia hugged Geedo's Bible to her chest. If Baba could entrust her with something as important as the family Bible, then Lesia had to make an important promise back.

"I'll take your Bible to Canada," she said slowly. "And I will learn to read. I'll also learn to write. I'll write to you, Baba. I will send the letter to your cousin, Dmytro. He can read it to you."

"Yes. Yes!" Baba's head bounced up and down.

"And when I write about the riches of Canada, you will change your mind and want to join us. I know you will."

Baba laid a gnarled hand on her shoulder. "And I know you will be strong, my darling, and you will keep the faith. Just remember, the flower is not always open. The sun does not always shine. But if your effort is true, your rewards will be sweet. It is my promise to you."

Chapter Three

Ah, Baba! I carried her memory across the ocean to Canada. I was determined to read and write for her. Determined to send for her. How could I know it was the last time I would see her?

I opened the Bible on the ship. I asked Ivan to teach me to read. But how could I read with the smell? You have not smelled such a smell! There are books written about how our people travelled across the ocean in search of a better life, but no book will tell you about that smell. Few alive remember it.

It was the stench of vomit and body odour. Of herrings and garlic and onions. Of hope and of fear and of death. It was a smell I had never smelled before. And never would again.

And yet it never really left me.

The sea was rough and that boat . . . it climbed mountains. Up and down, heaving and rolling, slamming into waves. Everyone was sick.

Hundreds of us. We were crammed together, below deck, the poor ones. For more than two weeks we travelled that way.

I had to put Baba's Bible away. There was Mama to care for. Sonia too.

The food they gave us was terrible, and we ran out of honey and kolachi, the special bread Baba had made. Someone had fish, but we were so sick and the fish smelled so bad that we went without. Sonia cried and cried from hunger. Once, someone took pity and shared with us two apples. Carefully we cut them up. I can still taste their juicy sweetness.

I saw two people die on that boat. When the old man died, the rain was coming so heavy they had to wait three days before they went up on deck and threw his body over. The little girl was different. She died at night and was gone by morning.

No book will tell you how it felt to watch a family mourn for a lost sister. A father. Words cannot tell of the fear in our eyes as we ate our last bit of bread and honey. Bozhe, Bozhe! Would we be the next to die?

When we landed, I gulped the air of my borrowed country like a thirsty man drinks water. It did not have the same pure smell as Shuparka but it smelled fine. We had arrived. Soon we would live rich, live free!

This is how we thought.

We had nothing. That money we worked so hard to save? Gone like smoke to men called agents who said they would help. Those men, they made big promises and they brought us to Canada, but every time we took a breath, they demanded more money. They overcharged for food . . . for currency . . . for examinations that were supposed to be free. They cheated us and others.

You know what it is to be poor and hungry and dirty? You do not know. All we had left was ten Canadian dollars for our land. Nothing more. Ach, our worries were big. But so were our dreams. And our best dream of all was the prairie.

The colonist train travelled many miles through rock. The books call it the Canadian Shield, yes? But the books do not tell of our wailing when we saw it. Many tears were shed as our train slowly crawled through the jagged wasteland. This was Canada? We thought we had been cheated. Lied to. Ivan and I were so angry we could not speak. Could not look at each other.

But then we saw it. The prairie.

The size of it silenced us all. Even the children. Mama said it was as though God had come to earth and proudly laid His best tapestry for all to see. It stretched on and on forever. Endless land. Boundless sky.

I wanted it to be pretty, the way Ivan had described it to me once. Golden wheat shimmering. He had read the words from a book. I had believed him.

There was no wheat. No shimmer. We had left behind the leafy aspens, the fragrant lindens, the blue periwinkles. Canada was a quilt of grey and brown—of snow and soil. Of lonely marshes and scrubby yellow grasses. Of small leafless trees that stretched like black skeletons to the sky.

"God has many tapestries," Mama told me, "and they are all beautiful." I thought of Baba saying the bees do not care if the flower is open only a little. They make do.

In my head, I made that prairie pretty. I saw rainbows sparkling in the melting snow. I saw food growing in the rich, brown soil . . . creeks swelling with a melt that would be our water . . . birds in thickets that would provide us with song. On distant hills, I saw green grass and tiny purple flowers and trees about to burst into leaf. I saw hope.

And soon I was in love. The prairie would give us land and food and dignity. A beautiful tapestry or a plain quilt, it did not matter. That prairie rolled and waved and dipped. It was endless. Boundless. Sun-kissed. Full of promise.

Just as we were.

April 22, 1914

Winnipeg, Manitoba

Canada was noisy and confusing!

Horses and buggies moved briskly past imposing brick buildings. Windows held goods Lesia didn't even recognize. Crowds of people milled about, immigrants as well as townsfolk. As the Magus family threaded its way down the sidewalk to the immigration hall, the smell of bread and fried onions floated out a doorway. Lesia's stomach growled. Bozhe, she was hungry! She hadn't eaten in almost two days.

"Dirty bohunks."

"Filthy peasant scum."

"Ignorant foreigners."

The English words made no sense, but that didn't stop Lesia from staring at the people who spoke. The men were clean-shaven and wore fine, dark coats, matching pants and impossibly tall hats. The women looked like fancy birds with their long, sweeping skirts, fitted white blouses and high, tittering voices.

"Dishonest and ill-mannered. They live ten to a room." A young girl giggled and pointed.

Lesia was suddenly ashamed of her dirty woollen skirt, her kerchief, the loose hemp blouse with its detailed embroidery.

"Stupid farmers. They can't even read."

Ivan scowled. He had a gift for languages; he was proud of the English he'd picked up on the ship.

"What are they saying?" she whispered as they went inside.

After making sure Mama and Sonia couldn't hear, Ivan said quietly, "That we are stupid and dirty and ignorant. That we are dishonest."

Lesia was shocked. She could have stayed at home and been ridiculed by Michal Stryk and the rest of the Polish nobility. "But I thought everyone was welcome in Canada."

"So did I until I boarded the train and I heard the truth." Ivan's eyes flashed in anger. "The British are welcome and so are the Northern Europeans, but they call us the unpreferred Continentals."

"But why?" Lesia asked.

Ivan shrugged. "Why do people hate? Some questions have no answers."

Papa overheard them. "Things will be different when we're with our own people in the Interlake," he said.

The official behind the long granite counter took one look at them and waved another man over. The man greeted them in familiar Ukrainian.

I hope this one doesn't demand money, like the one at the station in Quebec, Lesia thought. But this interpreter had a friendly, honest face. The Canadian official, on the other hand, had narrow lips, impatient eyes and seemed to dislike the Magus family on sight. In fact, Lesia realized as he barked orders at the interpreter, he seemed to dislike the Galician man too.

"He wants to know how much money you have." An embarrassed flush rose on the interpreter's face.

"Enough for our section of land," Papa said. In spite of being swindled four times during their trip, Papa still had the ten Canadian dollars he'd hidden in his sock.

"You need more," the interpreter replied swiftly, softly.

Papa's answer came just as quickly. "Then tell him we have more."

Beside her, Mama stiffened. Lesia gasped. Ivan gave her a sharp kick in the ankle. It was the first time in her life she could remember Papa lying! But what else could he do? They didn't have enough money to go back.

The Canadian official had more questions. "Where are you going?"

"The Interlake," Papa replied. "A place called Fraserwood."

The Canadian fastened a pair of small gold-rimmed glasses over the bridge of his nose, then picked up a piece of paper and studied it. Lesia held her breath.

"There is no land left there." The interpreter translated after the Canadian spoke.

"No!" She was light-headed, grateful for Ivan's hand on her arm.

It was Mama's turn to gasp.

"Most of our village is there." Papa spoke slowly, as though he were speaking to a young child. "They will make room for us."

The interpreter translated again. The Canadian official

shook his head. His response was clipped and harsh. His eyes flicked briefly over Ivan and Lesia before settling on Papa. It was that look! The same one that Michal Stryk had given her. Contempt mixed with scorn.

"There is no land left there," the interpreter told them again. He lowered his voice. "He speaks the truth, my friend. Trust me, you do not want—"

The Canadian official interrupted them. The Galician flushed again. "He says to tell you all the good land is gone. The land that's left is marginal. He says you should not have come. But that's not true," the interpreter rushed on. "You can claim a cancelled homestead in another area. There are still some left. Most are marginal, yes, but—"

"Marginal?" Mama interrupted him. "But how can we . . . ?" Her mouth moved but no words came. The colour drained from her lips. Her eyelids fluttered. She fell to the floor.

Sonia began to cry. Lesia grabbed her. People rushed forward. A grey-haired man with big, brown eyes and a thick, droopy moustache called out in Ukrainian for a doctor. Mama was lifted to an out-of-the-way corner and several people, including Papa, hovered around her.

Once she was propped up with a jacket and being tended to, the brown-eyed man who had called for help introduced himself. "Paul Korol," he said, extending a large, calloused hand to Papa. "Here to meet someone but they never arrived." Paul told them that he came from Bukovyna and had been in Canada thirteen years.

When Ivan asked him about marginal land, Paul said, "There's no way to know until you have a look. It might be marshy or rocky, or it might be fine. You need to see it. There are a few cancelled homesteads in my area, one south of us and two more north of Cooks Creek." Paul turned to Papa. "Come home with me," he suggested with a smile. "You'll have a place to stay while you have a look."

"Thank you, but no." Papa was stiff with embarrassment.

"Please," Paul said. "In Canada, immigrants help immigrants. If you were in my position, you would do the same."

"It's true, Papa," Ivan urged, "we would."

Papa was silent.

Lesia stared at the floor.

"You will stay with us," Paul announced firmly. "We would love to have you!"

* * *

Two weeks later, Papa's grin stretched from ear to ear. "It's ours!" He waved a small square of paper in front of Mama's face. "One quarter section of prairie land. Paid for with ten Canadian dollars." His voice held a touch of awe. "All ours. And in your name as well as mine, Ahafia."

Hollers of congratulations echoed through the farmhouse—the house south of Hazelridge belonging to Paul and his wife, Pearl, that had been home to them since they'd arrived in Manitoba.

Lesia and Ivan exchanged smiles. They'd been so scared when Mama had collapsed. The doctor said she had something called anaemia. She would need good food and lots of rest if she was going to carry the baby to term. The Korols were making sure she got both.

Lesia gave thanks to God every day for the goodness of the

Korols. Even though they had six children of their own, they cheerfully accommodated the Magus family and kept them full with what seemed to be a never-ending supply of food, much of which came from their vast farm.

"It's about seven miles northeast of Cooks Creek . . . about nineteen miles from here." Ivan tossed Sonia excitedly in the air. "There's a small shelter. And good soil." The tiny girl squealed with happiness.

It had taken Papa and Ivan more than a week to search out the best cancelled homestead they could claim. Papa had insisted on walking the countryside. Touching with his feet the soil of Canada, as he put it. This country was huge and it still amazed Lesia that everything was so far apart. Even Paul's farm was miles from his brother Andrew, who was his nearest neighbour.

"All we have to do is break thirty acres in the next three years and we'll be rich." Papa's eyes glittered with excitement. "Rich!"

Paul slapped him on the back. Andrew shook his hand.

"You make it sound so easy, my friend." Pearl soothed her youngest, baby Mary. "You forget that you'll water the soil with your blood, sweat and tears." Her smile showed the gap where her front teeth should have been.

Ivan laughed. "We'll do that seven times over for Canada. Won't we, Sonia?" He tossed his sister in the air again and she laughed even louder than before. Luka and Symon, the five-year-old twins, tugged on Ivan's sleeve. They wanted to be next.

Land of their *own*. Lesia cut the bread and tried to imagine. She could till and plant and harvest. Weave a skep, start a hive.

Pay back Master Stryk. Become a respected member of the community!

Paul's oldest daughter, Minnie, sidled up to Lesia. "It didn't take you long to figure out my Uncle Andrew has lots of money. Did you borrow his money for the land, like you borrowed his money for the doctor?"

Lesia swallowed her anger and looked away. She'd been so excited to learn Paul had a daughter near her age. But Minnie had disliked her from the moment they'd arrived.

"Minnie, come help your sisters put out the food!" Pearl called. Victoria and Anastasia, the two middle girls, were cheerfully helping their mother.

"Cooooooming, Mama!" Lowering her voice even more, she said, "You've already touched our bread, I wouldn't want you touching anything else." Her large, blue eyes swept over Lesia. "You are too dirty." Minnie flounced away.

The familiar prickle of embarrassment stung the back of Lesia's neck. To think she'd envied Minnie's long, blond hair and the elegant, factory-made skirts that rustled when she walked. Well, Minnie Korol may have been a pretty girl, but, as Baba would have said, the zluidni had touched her head. The zluidni were those nasty little creatures who lived in the forest and brought misery to everything they touched. And they had touched Minnie and tarnished her soul.

"Here you go, Lesia." Pearl handed her a steaming bowl of pyrohy. "You may put these on the table."

Minnie glared at her.

Besides the pyrohy, there was stewed rabbit, pickled beets, warm bread, jugs of milk and a platter of holubtsi, the cabbage rolls they ate back home at festive times, when they had enough cabbage and filling to make them. There was even sour cream to go with them. Lesia hadn't seen that in years!

"You'll need a milk cow, and oxen to clear the land," Paul was telling Papa as Lesia prepared a plate of food for Mama. "Or you could find someone with a ploughing outfit and pay him to do the work for you."

"We'll clear by hand." Papa waved away his concerns. "And we can do without milk for the summer. There's a creek full of water."

After handing Mama her plate, Lesia balanced Sonia on her knee and began to eat, listening quietly as the men continued to talk.

Andrew frowned. "I'll lend you the money for the oxen. And a cow. Pay me back when you can," he said. "This winter. Next summer even."

Andrew Korol was quieter than his brother Paul. Just twenty, he had thick black hair, a square determined chin and the saddest blue eyes Lesia had ever seen. He had married nine months ago and lost his young wife to consumption a few months later. According to Pearl, Andrew's half section of land was very profitable. It was thriving, but Andrew wasn't. That's why Pearl insisted he eat at least one meal a day with them.

Sonia grabbed at the smoked rabbit. Lesia broke off a small piece, handed it to her and watched Papa shake his head.

"You and your brother have done enough for us already," he said. "A team of oxen costs seventy dollars. And a cow is worth another twenty-five. I already owe the landowner in Shuparka one hundred rynskys." A muscle twitched nervously in Papa's cheek. "I can't borrow more money."

"You need to take care of your family." Andrew's eyes brushed over Lesia. "They're all you have."

She swallowed a small piece of warm, buttered bread. Andrew had to understand. They already owed him five dollars for the doctor's bill. And Papa was too proud to borrow more.

It was Ivan's turn to speak. "Once we clear the first ten acres, I'll find work. On the railroad maybe."

"Work is getting harder to come by," Paul said. "Wages are low. Working conditions in Winnipeg are terrible."

Ivan nodded. "I hear there's a movement afoot to organize the labourers."

Papa frowned. "Stay out of it, Ivan. Remember how you were watched in Shuparka."

"This isn't Ukraine, Papa. Canada is a democracy." Ivan looked amused. "Freedom of speech is allowed. Workers are allowed to express their opinions."

"True enough," Paul agreed with Ivan. "But there's repression here too. We must fight for what's right." The older man's eyes burned with conviction. "Just be careful. Look over your shoulder. Both of them."

The men laughed. Ivan rolled his eyes good-naturedly. Lesia and Mama exchanged grins. Ivan had obviously found a kindred spirit in Paul Korol. Thank goodness her brother would be too busy to become politically involved!

When everyone was finished eating, Lesia shyly asked Papa if she could see the deed to their land. She took it outside and found a quiet spot near an elm tree.

Heart racing, she unfolded the small slip of paper. With Ivan's help, she was learning to read, but nothing on this paper made sense. Lesia frowned and blinked. The characters were a mess of squiggles. Of course. They were in Canada now. The paper was written in English!

"I didn't know you could read."

Startled, Lesia looked up. Andrew had approached so silently she hadn't noticed. "Not English," she admitted, tucking the deed back into her apron. "Ukrainian. Ivan is teaching me."

Andrew was impressed. "Reading Ukrainian is just as important." He plucked a leaf and twirled it between his fingers. "I became a Canadian citizen last year, but in my heart I am still a Ukrainian."

Unlike your niece, Lesia thought, catching sight of Minnie twirling her younger brother, Luka, on the grass. Born just three days after her family had arrived in Canada, Minnie called herself a Canadian and seemed almost proud to deny her Ukrainian heritage.

Andrew changed the subject. "I wish you would consider taking a cow. And money for oxen."

Lesia shook her head. "My father's right. We already owe you for the doctor."

"Then perhaps you and your mother should stay here while Ivan and your father clear the land."

"We cannot impose any longer. Besides, I'm used to digging and cultivating." Just yesterday, Minnie had disdainfully told Lesia she had muscles as big as a horse's. Well, those muscles were going to be her salvation.

His blue eyes darkened. "You'll need plenty of food to see you through."

He was so serious. No doubt because of the death of his

wife. "I brought seeds from home," she reassured him. "I'll plant those."

He looked skeptical. "If the weather co-operates, they might produce. But the prairie can be harsh. Spring and summer are very short. Winter comes quickly and lasts a long time."

He couldn't know the hunger her family had endured for months on end in Shuparka, the hunger they'd travelled to Canada to escape. "I'll weave a skep. Set up a hive. We'll live off the land and put food by for winter." Where was Andrew's faith? Didn't he know if their efforts were true, their rewards would be sweet? "If we need more, I'll find work like Papa and Ivan." Across the yard, Minnie was watching them with a curious look on her face. Deliberately, Lesia turned her back.

"You cannot leave your mother alone. And you cannot take a chance with her health," he said softly. "She needs to eat."

Andrew was truly worried about them. Certainly he was right about one thing. Mama needed to eat to regain her strength.

Lesia gazed past the house and well, past the large garden plot and the thickets of berry brambles to the beckoning fields just waiting to be tilled and planted. Look at what the Korols had. It was impossible to starve in this land of plenty.

Wasn't it?

"If you won't take a cow, then let me buy you some potatoes and milk. Just enough to see you through the first few weeks. You can pay me back in a year's time."

"I don't know." Papa had been so angry when she'd borrowed from Master Stryk. He'd been very unhappy about borrowing five dollars for the doctor. He'd be furious if she borrowed again.

"I will make it a gift, then." Andrew smiled and his worry lines disappeared. He looked happier. Attractive. "Accept it for your mama's sake," he urged.

She hesitated. "A small gift, then. For Mama's sake." She smiled shyly. "We would be grateful to have it."

Papa would have to understand.

Chapter Four

May 10, 1914

The Magus homestead

"This is it!" With a sweep of his hand Ivan showed them the cancelled homestead they'd laid claim to. Papa stood proudly beside him.

Shifting Sonia from one hip to the other, Lesia stared at the scrubby poplars and aspens, the thickets of shrubs blooming with dainty flowers, the prairie grass that grew almost to her knees, and rock, so much rock!

It was unbroken and wild. But it was theirs. *All* theirs.

"Under these trees and rocks is black soil for growing. And over there is the creek, so we won't need to dig a well. Not yet," Papa added.

Lesia swallowed the lump in her throat. It would take them years to clear and plough and till and harvest. She had expected hard work, but they needed to grow food quickly, for nourishment as well as money. Beside her, Mama was stiff and still. She didn't dare look at her.

"The house is near the clearing," Ivan said, leading the way.

While the sun hinted at warmth, a light dusting of frost still clung to the ground. Lesia walked carefully, crunching over rocks and twigs, brushing against the prairie grass with her skirt. She thought of Paul's farm with its rolling fields of wheat, its immaculate thatched-roof cottage and its garden overflowing with spring greens and strawberries and small beet seedlings.

But the Korols had been in Canada thirteen years.

"That's it," Ivan pointed. "The house."

Mama gasped. Lesia's eyes widened in shock. It was nothing more than a burdei, a log and sod-brick dugout. It had a sloping, lopsided roof, a hole in one wall where a window was supposed to be and another larger hole waiting for a door. One side had been roughly plastered with clay, but tufts of grass poked out the other side like hair standing on end.

Lesia felt light-headed, faint. *Nothing* had prepared her for this.

"It's not much yet," Papa added quickly. "But with such a thick layer of soil, it will be cool in summer and warm in winter. And it's ours," he finished proudly.

"It's bigger than it looks," Ivan said.

Mama began to cry. "I want to go home." She sank to her knees. "Back to Ukraine."

"We won't be in it for long," Papa murmured as he comforted her. "A year at most."

"That . . . *thing*," Mama's hand shook as she pointed to the little dugout, "isn't fit for . . . for chickens."

Papa wrapped an arm around Mama's shoulder. "Once we clear the land and plant wheat, we'll build a proper house. With lots of windows." Lesia could hear the desperation in Papa's voice.

Clutching Sonia's head to her breast, Lesia looked around the clearing. There was a small clump of logs on one side and a clump of willows on the other.

"The creek's down there." Ivan gestured to his left.

Nodding, Lesia gazed beyond the clearing, looking for something, anything, to reassure her. But there was more scrub, more tree roots, more rock. Certainly not the great riches she had imagined.

What had they done?

Homesickness rolled through her. If only she could see the sun setting behind the church in Shuparka one last time. Smell the plum blossoms. Hug Baba. They'd had no respect in Ukraine, and life there was hard, but at least it was predictable. In Canada, nothing was predictable. And something told her respect would be a long time coming.

In the far distance was the neighbouring farm, which, according to Andrew, belonged to an Englishman. Ribbons of rich, black soil stretched to the blue horizon. That land had been rock and trees and scrubby bush once too, Lesia thought. Perhaps this wasn't so bad after all.

Lesia followed Ivan inside. The burdei was dark and dreary, even with the small sliver of sun shining through the tiny window onto the dirt floor. A limp mound of hay and a tattered piece of a blanket were shoved into the corner, a visible reminder of those who had lived here before. Lived here and left.

Ivan ran a trembling hand through his hair. Hope seemed to fade from his face. "We've come halfway around the world in search of a dream that has all the makings of a nightmare," he said gloomily.

"Don't say that," Lesia said sharply. Since they'd left Shuparka, Ivan had been the strongest of them all. Not once had he given in to second thoughts, to fear, or to pity. And his strength was her strength. "There's hope in Canada, Ivan. We will *earn* respect. We will be valued. In Ukraine, we were worthless peasants. They took away our land. We were starving."

Ivan shook his head. "This all looked fine last week. But when I see it through your eyes . . . through Mama's eyes . . ." He peered out the small window and sighed. "I don't know."

She would *not* let Ivan have regrets. "Paul's farm was virgin soil once, too. And look what he did with it." Lesia was filled with a renewed sense of purpose. A sense of adventure. "Look at this. We have 160 acres. It's *ours!* We can turn it into something, I know we can."

Ivan turned to face her. "It's going to be much harder than I thought. And it's going to take longer."

Sonia squirmed in her arms and Lesia put her down. "I know," she agreed softly. "But every hour of every day is going to be worth it! Every sore muscle. Remember Slavko and Geedo? Remember our vow?"

"That no one in our family would suffer from hunger again." Ivan repeated the words slowly. "That we would not allow ourselves to be treated badly. That we would not lose any more land." His voice took on renewed strength. "That we would live rich, live free." The look of despair slowly faded from his face.

"Canada is giving us a chance, Ivan." Lesia remembered Michal Stryk sneering down his nose at her. And those nasty people outside the immigration hall. But surely not everyone was like that? "There's no aristocracy in Canada. People are equal here. We can follow our dreams." She walked over to the thick window ledge where Sonia was peering outside. "Like Baba said, the bees work long and hard, and they don't complain. We shouldn't either. We have land. A place to sleep. I'm learning to read. Life is already good," she told him with a smile. "And it's only going to get better."

Lesia sliced forcefully through the soil with the spade. One hundred and sixty acres was a *good* thing. But why did a good thing have to take so much work? In Shuparka, digging and cultivating had been as simple as folding pyrohy dough. Years of cultivation had left that soil light and easy to turn. Canadian soil, on the other hand, was thick and dark and heavy—not used to human hands.

But it was beautiful, Lesia thought, as she brought the spade down on a large clump of earth. It crumbled, and a blister on her palm popped. She could feel the pus ooze and slide against the spade handle. Fleetingly she remembered the words she had said to Ivan not long ago. *Every hour of every day and every sore muscle. Worth it.* As stiff and sore and blistered as she was, it had been worth it already.

Straightening, she smiled at Sonia, who was picking up small rocks and piling them near the dugout, where they'd be sorted later. Mama was plastering the burdei with the clay they'd found in a pit on the east side of their land.

She wasn't well, Lesia thought as she watched her slow, laborious movements. Their diet didn't agree with her. She was having trouble keeping food down. Especially gopher.

Robins twittered the last of their daylight song. The setting sun threw a shadowy haze of pink over the burdei and the white muslin that hung in the doorway. Inside, Baba's kylym had been hung. The window ledge held the picture of the Blessed Virgin, Geedo's cross and their small bottle of holy water. Fresh hay had been laid for bedding; tree stumps gave them a place to sit.

Turning, Lesia caught sight of the two bee skeps she'd woven out of willow twigs. The bees hadn't arrived yet, but she was hopeful they'd come. There was a path to the creek now, they had made a good start at clearing their first acre of land, and the garden—if she could finish the digging tonight—would be planted tomorrow.

Amazing, Lesia thought as she went back to work, how much they had accomplished in just a few weeks.

"Heave hooooo!" Ivan yelled as another tree fell. Sonia dropped the small rock she was carrying and clapped. Papa and Ivan dragged a large aspen to the woodpile. A woodpile! She shook her head in wonder. Anyone having so much wood in Shuparka would be rich indeed. Here, wood was pushed aside in favour of cleared land.

One more thing to get used to in this strange place.

"Hungry, Lessie."

"Soon, Sonia." Taking advantage of every bit of natural light meant they didn't eat dinner until it was dark.

Reminding Sonia to stand back, Lesia lifted her arms and smashed the spade against the soil, visualizing with each stroke how it would look planted with food—nourishing food Mama was familiar with. It was a good spot for a garden, near enough to the creek that they wouldn't have far to haul water.

"She's sick again," Ivan muttered as he joined Lesia.

She looked up in time to see Papa attending to Mama. "We have to do something." She bit her lip.

"I'm going to leave soon. Find work. Buy flour and supplies."

"You can't," she said sharply.

Sonia looked up and pouted. "Lessie okay?"

After reassuring the child, Lesia turned back to her brother. "We need to build a root cellar. And an oven. And we have to clear more land." She watched Papa settle Mama by the fire near the burdei.

"We're almost out of food."

"We have a few potatoes left. We've got wild greens for soup. And the creek—"

"I haven't trapped one fish in that creek," Ivan interrupted. "I'm sure that neighbour has dammed it and is taking the spoils for himself."

"Well, there's rabbit and gopher. Even if Mama can't eat it, the rest of us can. I'm seeding tomorrow. There will be vegetables from the garden soon and wild strawberries too. Andrew says they're sweeter than candy."

Ivan scowled. "Andrew! If only he'd given us a sack of flour instead of those silly gifts!"

"Ivan!" She was shocked at his lack of gratitude. "Don't say that. It's enough that Pearl and Paul gave us eggs to eat and hay to sleep on. And Andrew gave us those potatoes and milk and soap and candle supplies."

"As well as paper and a pencil," he said with a grimace. "They won't keep us from starving."

She stuck her chin into the air. "You do not question the generosity of a gift. You accept it with gratitude."

"There are more important things than reading," he muttered.

Learn to read and write, Andrew had said when he'd handed her the paper and pencil. Then, when your farm is productive, you'll be rich *and* educated. Exactly, Lesia had retorted with a grin.

Ivan smacked his hand against his knee and leaned close. "I know you're staying positive, just like Baba said. But Mama can't eat gopher. She needs bread and potatoes to nourish the baby. It's going to take time for the garden to grow. We have to buy a sack of flour, a bushel of potatoes." Ivan's voice dropped even lower. "And we need horses or oxen. Maybe a plough. Paul was right. This land is hard to break. We need money, Lesia."

She stared at him. "I know."

The colour was fading from the sky. Soon it would be dark. They were silent then, lost in their own thoughts. Lesia was the first to speak.

"Perhaps we should borrow money for a team of oxen, like

Andrew suggested," she said slowly. "We could get a cow or some chickens, too. Sell the eggs or the cream. We could start paying off our debts and produce food at the same time."

"Papa will never go for it," Ivan said.

With a jolt of alarm, Lesia noticed how thin her brother was getting. His cheekbones were sticking out from his face like wings sticking out from a bird. If Ivan got too skinny, he'd be too weak to work the land. She had to do something. "I'll convince him," Lesia promised as her brother shook his head and walked away.

They had only a few minutes of light left. Lesia quickly resumed her digging. Behind her, Sonia babbled in her high-pitched, singsong voice. "Gopher," she said happily.

"Yes, yes." Lesia didn't bother turning around. If she stopped to watch every gopher that came along, she'd never get anything done. "Take that last rock to the pile now. It's almost time for soup."

"Gopher, Lessie. Gopher."

"I see." She gave a cursory glance over her shoulder, just enough to satisfy her little sister.

"Pretty!" Sonia babbled, pointing to a black-and-white creature a few feet away.

Lesia looked back. Fleshier than either a rabbit or a gopher, the animal had tiny black eyes, glossy black fur and a thick white stripe running down its back and curling up the length of a long, fluffy tail. "That's not a gopher, Sonia." Gophers, or prairie dogs, as Andrew had called them, were a dull grey-brown.

"Yes!" Sonia stomped her foot against the ground. "Gopher."

Lesia watched the small animal walk daintily around the pile of rocks. "But if it's not a gopher, maybe Mama could eat it for dinner," she murmured softly.

"Pretty gopher," Sonia chirped again. She picked up a stick and tapped the ground in front of her. The creature turned. Its tail straightened. A low hissing sound travelled through the air.

Sonia's bottom lip quivered. "Not nice gopher," she pouted.

"The gopher is tired now. He doesn't want to play. Go talk to Mama." She pushed the little girl towards the fire.

The animal ambled over the rocks and headed slowly towards the scrub close to the creek, its white stripe making it clearly visible in the twilight.

It would be easy to catch! And meaty. More than enough for five.

She'd have to use her spade, Lesia thought, following it. Creep up behind it and smash it on the head.

A picture of those innocent black eyes flashed through her mind. Could she do it?

She had to. Their very survival depended on food.

Closer and closer Lesia crept. If it knew it was being followed, it paid no attention. She watched in fascination as its black-and-white tail grew straighter and straighter, until it was pointing directly into the air, like the flag on the ship they'd taken in Hamburg.

Just a few more steps. Clutching the spade in both hands, she raised it over her head.

The creature hissed. Its back arched in warning.

It had to be now! Taking a deep breath, Lesia struck hard. And missed.

Suddenly her eyes began to sting and burn. Her nose and mouth filled with an odour so foul it made tears run down her cheeks. Bozhe, Bozhe, she was choking!

A piercing scream sliced through the air. Rubbing furiously at her face and gasping for breath, Lesia realized the scream had come from an outraged Sonia. Her sister had followed her.

Chapter Five

Ivan and Papa were still laughing the next morning.

"Imagine eating *that!*" Ivan said. They rocked back and forth with laughter over their bowls of soup. Paul had told the two men about the black-and-white creatures that could turn the air foul with a single spray, but Papa and Ivan had neglected to tell the women to watch for them. And, in spite of Lesia's efforts to wash their clothes and scrub their skin, the putrid smell clung to them like an unwelcome guest.

Chuckling, Papa headed out to the garden. Lesia grabbed the seeds she'd brought from Shuparka and quickly followed him. Perhaps his good mood would make him more agreeable.

"No. Absolutely not." He'd crossed his arms and frowned before she'd even finished asking the question.

"But we're down to the last few potatoes. Mama was sick

again this morning." She set the seeds on the ground. "We need to buy flour. And Sonia needs fresh milk."

"No more debt, Lesia. Absolutely not." His jaw was set in that all too familiar look.

"But this debt will pay for itself." She repeated the argument she'd given Ivan. "We'll have food to eat, and eggs or cream to sell. We can buy supplies. We can pay Andrew the five dollars we owe him. And start paying back Master Stryk."

"No more debt," Papa said again.

"We have to do something."

"Ivan and I are going to see if we can find work on the railroad." He wouldn't look at her.

"But you know the promise we made to the Canadian government," Lesia said. "We have to show improvements on the land. We have to break ten acres this summer. Or build a house. Mama's in no condition to work. And I can't do it all by myself." A lone bee droned near her ear. Lesia brushed it in the direction of her bee skep.

"Do the best you can. I won't be gone for long. I'll help you when I get back."

"Why don't I go out to work?" she asked. "I'll dig seneca roots and sell them, or work as a hired hand. You can stay here."

Papa shook his head. "Ivan and I can make more money." This time he did look at her. "I'm sorry."

"If you'd let me buy a cow, I could make money too," Lesia said impatiently. The bee was back. She cupped her hand around it and nudged it towards the skep again. "Or bees. I'm waiting for a swarm to settle, but Andrew said there are people who sell entire colonies."

"No more debt!" Papa glared at her. "You borrowed from Master Stryk against my wishes. You borrowed from Andrew and the Korols against my wishes."

"I didn't borrow from Andrew or the Korols," she retorted. "That food and those . . . those . . . extra things were gifts!"

"We must pay them back." Papa's jaw was set. "And no more borrowing. That's my final word, Lesia."

Defiantly, she stared back at him. "Then at least clear one more acre before you go. And dig a root cellar. Please!"

Her father nodded. "Very well," he said slowly. "But then we leave."

* * *

After days of rain, Lesia should have been cheered to wake up and see the morning sun glowing through the white muslin in the doorway. It was warm and bright—the last day of May and the first dry day in a week. But all she could think about was the hollow pit in her stomach. The few potatoes that were left had been set aside for Mama and Sonia. Papa, Ivan and Lesia were living on soup—a thin, watery blend of gopher and rabbit bones, potato peelings and greens—or whatever they could hunt.

And with the rain, hunting had been meagre.

"Ivan and I are going to start digging the root cellar today," Papa told her. "You check the traps and then work the land south of the vegetable garden."

Lesia picked up her tools and headed outside. The air was early-morning fresh. She lifted her face and let the sun's warmth wash over her.

Dearest Baba, are you enjoying the same sun in Shuparka?

While she welcomed the sun, the rain had at least given her a little reprieve. It had prevented the men from leaving and had given her time to weave a few baskets and practise her reading and writing. Soon she would be able to write to Baba, she thought, coming to a sudden stop beside the garden.

The rain had also made the sunflowers and cabbage sprout! Lesia grinned. The tiny seedlings marched in rows, along with beets and hemp and something called kale. A hearty green, Paul had called it when he'd given them the seed. Soon they would be eating their own food. Mama would be so pleased!

Scrambling down the bank to the shallow creek, she took a breath and waded into the icy water. The rain had made the water level rise; it was deeper than usual. She grappled for the trap, found it and pulled. Nothing! With a grimace of disgust, she reset it and tossed it back into the water. The water was good for bathing and drinking, she thought as she filled the tin can she had brought from the dugout, but not so good for fishing. Maybe Ivan was right. Maybe their neighbour was trapping all the fish for himself.

The rabbit trap was empty too, sprung by another coyote that had left bits of fur and dried blood behind. If only Mama could manage to eat gopher, Lesia thought as she headed for the south field, the grass rustling against her knees as she brushed against it. If only they had more potatoes. Or some flour.

In the distance was the farm she had admired the day they'd first arrived. She could see a man—their neighbour—checking his cows. A baby calf. He looked up. She waved her arm and yelled out a greeting.

He turned away.

He hadn't seen her, Lesia decided as she picked up her axe. Perhaps he didn't want to see her?

There are many Michals in the world, and they would like us to live beneath them. Baba's words floated through her mind. But Baba had also said that all people are equal in the eyes of God.

Canada would give Lesia a chance to prove that and more.

The rain had left the ground moist and heavy, and with each stroke of the axe, grass and soil and flower petals rained into the air, a colorful blend of purple violets and orange lilies and white lupins.

On and on she worked, hacking and chopping, separating rock from soil, until the sun was high in the sky. By then, she was dripping with sweat and her muscles, well rested after days of inactivity, were tightly knotted. She reached for the tin of water she'd taken from the creek. It was all she could do not to empty the can completely.

Her stomach growled with hunger. Bozhe, to sit in the shade of the dugout and eat a real meal instead of watery soup! Instead, she sat by her rock pile, dipped two fingers into the tin of water and dabbed her cheeks . . . the nape of her neck. Aaaaaahhh. Warm but refreshing.

There was a rustle from behind. Lesia froze.

It was an animal. Was it a skunk?

Putting the tin down, she pulled herself to a crouch and slowly turned. Her body was stiff; she was ready to run. There was another rustle. Then a flash of brown-gold. It was a prairie chicken.

Mama loved fowl! Maybe, just maybe, if she was fast, she could kill it. Lesia grabbed a large rock and aimed.

Feathers flew. A howl of protest sounded from the innocent bird. Stunned, it thrashed about and attempted flight.

Grabbing her axe, Lesia lifted it over her head and lunged forward. She struck out once, twice, unsure if she was hitting the ground, the bird or both. But she would *not* let it get away. The prairie chicken flapped and screeched. Bile rose and lodged in Lesia's throat. She had never killed anything in her life. The closest she'd come was plucking feathers from the old hens in Shuparka.

Finally, the creature was still. Dead.

Tossing the axe aside, she forced her feet to move forward, to look at what she'd done. Her blows had severed the chicken's neck. She had decapitated it. But her other blows must have hit the ground because the body was in one piece.

It was a good size. More than enough to feed five.

Swallowing the lump in her throat, she bent down. The nearby grass was splattered with droplets of blood. More blood pooled on the ground under the bird's neck, and blood trickled through the feathers of the bird's wing like beet juice staining a piece of bread.

Lesia reached out. The bird twitched and flopped. Horrified, she jumped back. Of course it was moving. That happened after birds were slaughtered. Frowning at her foolishness, she forced her hand forward. There was its head, off to the side. And its eyes watching her. *Don't look.*

She lifted it by its feet. They were slick. Warm. More blood drained to the ground. Lesia swayed. She would *not* be sick. She took a deep, steadying breath. *You must do this.*

Anxious to show the others her catch, she began to run. The chicken flapped and splattered blood on her apron, but Lesia's squeamishness was gone. Tonight they would eat a prairie chicken. It was going to taste wonderful roasted over the fire!

"Look," she yelled when the dugout was in sight. "Look."

Sonia saw her first. Her scream of delight alerted Mama and Papa.

"What have we here?" Papa beamed.

Lesia lowered the chicken and allowed Sonia to touch the feathers that were clean. "Dinner," she said proudly.

Mama looked incredulous. "You killed that yourself?"

She grinned. "There was no one else to kill it for me, Mama." She looked around the clearing. "Where's Ivan?"

Papa pointed.

She followed the direction of Papa's finger. Ivan was standing behind the dugout, where the root cellar was going to be. And he wasn't alone.

"We have company," Papa said.

Chapter Six

"His name is Wasyl Goetz and he's looking for work," Papa explained. "He needs money."

Didn't they all? She studied the man. He was taller than Ivan, with broad shoulders, sandy brown hair and a thin stubble of beard.

Ivan glanced over, saw the prairie chicken and grinned. Wasyl Goetz turned. His eyes widened. She recognized the desperate yearning in his eyes: hunger.

The two of them walked towards her, and Lesia tried not to stare. His sheepskin coat was worn, his pants were torn at the knees, his shoes were held together with string. He carried a faded red blanket tied into a bundle, and a rifle over his shoulder. What she could do with a rifle!

"Well done," Ivan said. "We'll eat plenty tonight."

An embarrassed silence fell and Wasyl Goetz stared at the ground.

"You'll stay, of course," Mama said to him.

"Thank you." He looked up, smiled shyly. "I have a few potatoes in my bag. You would like to cook those to go with the bird, yes?"

Extra potatoes! Lesia could scarcely stop herself from laughing out loud. Mama could make pyrohy.

"You keep them," Mama said generously. "Let us feed you."

Mama did make pyrohy—out of the last of their own potatoes. Lesia refused to think about what they would eat tomorrow. Instead, after the bird was strung up over the fire, she listened to Wasyl tell Ivan and Papa about his experiences searching for work.

There was little left on the railroad, and it was tough in the city, too. Thousands of Ukrainians had marched in Winnipeg demanding jobs. "They yell over and over again—work or bread, work or bread." He shook his head. "There is so little work that men are organizing in protest. And things are just as bad in the homeland." Wasyl shook his head. "It's not a pretty picture."

"How so?" Ivan asked.

"Word is the army is mobilizing on the border between Russia and Galicia," he said. "Talk of war is at an all-time high."

"If there is a war, what will that mean?" Lesia asked.

Papa reached over and adjusted the spit that held the chicken. "War is never good." His eyes had a sad, faraway look. He'd watched his father march off to fight in the Austro-Prussian War. It had been the last time he'd seen the man alive.

"War may not be good, but it always brings opportunity." Ivan's blue eyes darkened with excitement. "And that can be a good thing."

"Absolutely." Wasyl nodded vigorously. "War means Ukrainians can fight to regain their homeland. And maybe the Canadian men will join up—that'll mean more work for those left behind." He and Ivan shared a grin.

Though she sat in the warmth of the fire, a cold chill crept down Lesia's back. This talk of war was frightening her.

"Enough!" Papa said firmly. "Canada is a peaceful country. There will be plenty of opportunity without war."

"There's no opportunity in the city," Wasyl said again. "That's why I'm walking to Teulon. A farmer there is looking for two men to till and plant his field."

Papa and Ivan exchanged looks. "Just two?" Papa asked.

Wasyl nodded. "An Icelandic fellow who has a half section and enough money to take on two men for a month. Met him in Winnipeg."

"How do you know the position will still be open when you get there?" Ivan asked.

"He's holding it for me." Wasyl flexed one arm and chuckled. "I have a reputation as a horse! I work harder than two men together. I was doing pretty well until my last job. That boss was harsh. He worked me fourteen hours a day and fed me just once. At least I was in the barn with the cows. After he went to bed, I'd fill up on milk."

The three men laughed.

"How much did you make?" Lesia asked.

The laughter ended abruptly. Papa frowned. Ivan looked disgusted. "That's none of your business," her brother said.

"I don't mean to pry." She appealed directly to Wasyl. "But if I could go out and make some money, I'd like to know how much to ask for."

"It depends what you do." Wasyl glanced at her small shoulders. She could feel herself flushing as he studied her skinny arms. "I worked the fields. But as a woman . . ." he hesitated, "you could maybe find work plastering ovens."

Lesia felt slighted. She wasn't as fast as Papa or Ivan, but she was just as capable. "I work our field every day. And I killed tonight's chicken." *Without a rifle*, she added silently.

"You're not going anywhere," Papa said firmly.

She ignored him. "How much for working the fields?"

"Lesia!" Papa's voice climbed in warning.

Wasyl didn't seem to mind. "A few dollars a day, less by the month. But women aren't usually hired to work the fields. Try plastering. You could make fifty cents a day."

"I can work the field as well as any man." She kicked angrily at the ground. What she could do with two dollars a day! Pay a little to Master Stryk. Buy food. Save some for chickens. Or a cow.

"It doesn't matter, Lesia, because you'll be staying here with Mama and Sonia."

"You never minded me working in Shuparka." She crossed her arms defiantly.

Papa's eyebrows stretched across his forehead. "This isn't Shuparka."

True enough. Canada was nothing at all like the homeland.

By the end of the first week in June, the men were ready to leave.

"Take good care of yourself, little one. And of Mama and Sonia." Papa smiled down at her.

Nodding, she tugged nervously on the corner of her apron. "Of course."

Mama helped Ivan tie his few belongings into a square of white muslin. Wasyl Goetz played with Sonia. Lesia and Papa were alone.

"The root cellar is finished. We have an oven now. The garden is starting to grow. And thanks to Wasyl, you have a little fresh meat to keep you going."

"Yes." She nodded. Wasyl Goetz was both a blessing and a curse. A blessing because he worked so hard. But a curse for the same reason. In the week he'd stayed with them, he'd helped Papa finish the root cellar, lent a hand plastering the oven and helped Ivan clear another acre of land. Then yesterday he'd killed another prairie chicken, two rabbits and a gopher. But with the work done and freshly killed meat on hand, Papa had gained a false sense of security. Now he thought it was fine to leave.

"How soon will you be back?" she asked. "We still have eight acres left to clear."

"If I can, I'll be back in a few weeks with some food," Papa promised. "Or I'll send money. But you heard Wasyl. Work is getting harder to find. We must make some money before winter. Be strong, Lesia. For Mama and for Sonia."

Instead of encouraging her, Papa's words reminded her of the enormous responsibility ahead. Clearing the rest of the land. Preparing the fields. Caring for the others. Especially for

Mama, who was really slowing down. If Baba were here to help her, she wouldn't feel so alone. Or so afraid.

"Let me go with Ivan and Wasyl," she pleaded again. "Between Ivan and me, we could make enough to see us through the winter. And you could stay here with Mama and Sonia." The thought of Papa leaving truly frightened her. "*Please*, Papa. *Please*?"

"Where is that faith you're always talking about?" Papa grinned and gave her shoulder an encouraging squeeze. "You can do this, Lesia. Mama can't help with the heavy work, but there are plenty of things she can do. She can cook, she can weave baskets from willow. And you're reading Geedo's Bible now. That will bring you comfort during the lonely nights. Be strong, daughter. Strong and brave. The rewards will be sweet."

She turned away. She didn't want Papa to see her cry. But she couldn't hide her misery from Ivan when he and Mama joined them a few minutes later.

"Everything will work out," Ivan said softly.

She said nothing. Instead she watched as Wasyl walked slowly towards them, with Sonia perched happily on his shoulders.

The blessing and the curse.

Wasyl had promised Papa that he'd recommend him to the Icelandic farmer who needed a second hand. Surely, he'd said, the Icelandic farmer would know someone who could use Ivan's help. Those were good things. But he'd also spent many hours talking with Ivan about the injustices faced by the immigrants. Not only were some of the English-speaking Canadians calling the immigrants nasty names just because they were different, but some newspapers even referred to them as disease-ridden people with a low standard of living. It was enough to put the old spark in Ivan's eyes. The spark that had been there when he'd tried to organize the men in Shuparka.

"Don't do anything silly, Ivan," she demanded. "Promise me!"

Ivan looked indignant. "Silly? What do you mean, silly? I'm going out to make money. To pay off our debts and buy provisions."

Sonia and Mama were hugging Papa. All three were fighting back tears. Lesia couldn't look.

"You know what I mean," she hissed. "Don't get involved in politics. Put your energy where we need it most. In making money."

Ivan cocked an eyebrow and gave her a mock salute. "Any other marching orders?"

"Bring home a cow." She grinned slightly. "A fat, brown one. And don't be gone long. We have land to clear."

Chapter Seven

June 15, 1914

The Magus homestead

Wasyl Goetz was the first visitor to the Magus homestead, but not the last. After the men left, the weather warmed and the peddlers arrived. First there was a heavily bearded man carrying an overstuffed backpack. While Mama gave him a drink of water, Sonia and Lesia drooled over pocket knives, bandanas and bolts of brightly coloured cotton. When the next man came, Lesia was ready. She pulled out several of her willow baskets and bartered them for a needle and a few eggs. That gave her an idea.

"I'm going to see our English neighbour," Lesia said one afternoon when Mama and Sonia were settling for a nap. "Maybe I can trade him for some milk and butter." She tucked two of her best baskets under her arm and headed for the creek, determined to follow it to the adjoining farm. Ivan had warned her that prejudice was rampant, but surely neighbours could get along.

Though Lesia had been very careful with the meat Wasyl had killed, they only had a little potted rabbit and a few strips of dried prairie chicken left. And while the seedlings were up in the garden and she was using some of them in soup, she had to let most of the plants grow so they'd have enough for winter.

In spite of the fact that Mama's belly bulged with the baby, she was painfully thin and weak. Sonia constantly complained of hunger. Lesia herself was often ravenous, no doubt because of all the heavy work she was doing. She was determined to clear another acre before Papa returned. But she needed more food to keep up her strength.

It was blessedly cool in the shade of the towering elms. A small bird flitted from one branch to the next. Dearest Baba had loved the birds . . . and the bees. If only Baba were here to give her a hug. Instead, she had Geedo's Bible to hug and Baba's promise to remember. *Let the effort be true, and the rewards will be sweet.*

The sight of the dam drove the words from her mind.

Ivan had been right! Shocked, Lesia stared at the crudely constructed barrier of branches and planks and rocks that stretched the width of the stream. Craning her neck, she could see a couple of fish swimming lazily in the clear water on the other side. On her *neighbour's* property.

With an uneasy feeling in her stomach, she clutched the baskets to her chest, climbed the bank, gave the dam a wide berth and hurried on. A man who prevented the fish from swimming downstream to their homestead might not be all that happy to see her.

When his house was in sight, she left the protection of the trees and walked purposefully across the field, feeling hot and vulnerable in the midday sun. She was almost to his barn when a yell stopped her.

Whirling around, Lesia dropped one of her baskets. By the time she had retrieved it, he was in front of her, a barrel-chested man with a sharp, weasel-like face.

He yelled and gestured angrily with his arms, practically spitting out words she had come to recognize.

Bohunk. Dirty peasant.

She pretended not to understand. Instead she ignored the flush of heat crawling up the back of her neck, held out her baskets and said, "You buy . . . for milk."

His voice rose, his eyes narrowed, he took a step forward.

Heart pounding, Lesia fled.

She didn't stop running until she'd reached the protection of the trees. And she didn't stop walking until she'd reached the dam.

Angry and humiliated, she sank onto the ground beside the creek. How could people be so cruel? Where was the respect she had come to Canada to find?

She stared at the dam, wishing she could break it into a thousand pieces, destroy it and all the hate and prejudice in the world at the same time.

She didn't dare.

Did she?

She glanced over her shoulder to make sure she was alone,

removed her shoes and stockings and dangled her feet in the water. She didn't have to destroy it, *exactly*. She edged closer, touching one plank experimentally with her toes. It gave way, bouncing back when she eased up on the pressure.

Hiking her dress up to her waist, Lesia waded into the water, giving the bottom of the dam a sharp kick with her foot. Two branches moved. The left side of the dam slid down a few inches. There was a change in the current. The water was flowing through.

But was the opening big enough for fish to get through?

Reassuring herself that she was still alone, Lesia gave some of the lower rocks a hard kick. *Craaack!* The whole structure shifted slightly; she could feel the water flowing more strongly.

She hurried out of the water, eyeing the dam critically as she grabbed her shoes and stockings, her two baskets. It didn't look *that* different, not really, just a little lower in the water, a little more uneven.

Hopefully, the only ones to notice would be the fish.

* * *

They ate fresh fish for several weeks. What they couldn't eat, they dried and put up for winter. Mama grew more energetic, Sonia stopped whining, and Lesia went to bed at night with a full belly.

By the beginning of July, however, the traps in the creek were suddenly empty and the fish stopped coming. The break in the dam had obviously been repaired. They were back to careful rationing and foraging, living on wild strawberries and gopher. Mama grew quiet; Sonia became fretful. Lesia worked the land by day and practised writing by night. Her bedtime came long after Mama and Sonia had fallen asleep. With her stomach cramped by hunger, she would pray for Papa to return . . . for bees to settle in the skeps. Only then would she shut her eyes and fall into a restless sleep. A sleep dominated by dreams of beloved Baba, whose arms overflowed with bread and milk and butter and eggs.

* * *

"Look Lessie, wiggles!" Sonia giggled and held out a thick green worm.

Lesia turned from the empty skeps to stare at the pale insect. It was the same worm that was munching on their cabbages. Yesterday, the leaves had been sturdy and upright. Today, they were ragged and full of holes.

Bozhe! If the bugs destroyed the cabbages, they'd have nothing left for winter.

"Here, darling. Play with this." She handed Sonia a stick, and as soon as her sister was occupied, she took the worm and squished it under her heel. Then she bent down and searched through the damaged cabbage. She killed three more pale green worms.

Like them, the garden was struggling to survive. Two weeks into July and there was no sign of relief from the hot summer weather. Not a cloud in the sky, not a drop of rain in sight. The water level in the creek was dangerously low. Drinking water was their first priority; watering the garden came second. The plants were stressed, and the bugs loved that.

"Hungry," Sonia whined.

"Yes, I know." She pulled off the damaged leaves and set them aside for soup.

"Tummy hurts." Sonia threw the stick on the ground and began to pout. "Want berries."

"We'll go looking soon."

"Berries noooooow!" The child started to cry.

Lesia sighed. She was so used to the hunger pangs, she hardly felt them any more. Mama had stopped complaining as well. But not Sonia. Her little sister was constantly hungry. To make matters worse, she also had a cold. And now Mama was complaining of a sore throat.

"Come here." She pulled Sonia towards her and wiped away her tears. "How about we play a game."

"A game?" Sonia looked suspicious.

"You help me look for those little green worms, and if we find lots, we'll build them a little house with sticks."

Sonia grinned. "Okay. They my friends, Lessie."

"You look now," she encouraged. She wasn't sure what she'd say in the morning when Sonia found the small green worms gone; today, she just needed to get them out of the garden.

"Found one!" Sonia yelled.

She watched her sister lay the offending green bug near the rest. Just then, Mama appeared in the clearing. She seemed to be struggling under the weight of the water cans.

Lesia began to run. "I told you I would go for water," she yelled.

Mama shook her head slightly, opened her mouth to speak and then slowly crumpled to the ground. The tin cans flew out of her hands, spraying water in all directions.

Lesia flew to her side. "Mama!"

She had landed on her back. Water plastered her dress. Her round belly jutted into the air. Her face was potato white. Sooty black circles were etched under her closed eyes.

"Mama! Mama?" Lesia touched her mother's forehead. It was cool, not warm. Her chest was rising and falling. She was breathing. Bozhe! She was breathing.

"Lessie, Mama okay?" Sonia called from the garden.

"Mama's fine, darling. You play now." *Papa, where are you when I need you!?*

After what seemed like an eternity, Mama opened her eyes. "I must have tripped," she whispered.

"You didn't trip at all," Lesia said fiercely. "You fainted. It's the anaemia again, isn't it?"

Mama struggled to sit up but the baby set her off balance.

"Don't stand yet," Lesia ordered. "Sit a while." When the colour had finally returned to Mama's face, she gently asked, "Is the baby okay?"

"The baby's fine." Mama rubbed her belly reassuringly before grabbing Lesia's arm and struggling to her feet. "Carrying a child has never been easy for me. And it's harder still now. But there's no sense complaining. Nothing can be done to change things. As God ordains, so it shall be."

Nothing can be done to change things. She had grown up with Mama saying those words. It may have been true in Ukraine, but it certainly wasn't true in Canada.

"You're wrong, Mama." She watched Sonia playing with her stick and the worms. "I can go to work plastering."

When Mama protested, Lesia held up her hand and stopped her. "Remember what Pearl said? When the weather turns cold, it will be impossible to travel the land and find work, never mind walk twelve miles to the store in Hazelridge. If I leave now, I can earn enough for flour and potatoes, maybe even a few eggs. I'll take my baskets too. Maybe I'll sell some." Surely not everyone was like their neighbour.

Mama looked panicked. "I need you here. There's Sonia to care for. And I'm too weak to work the land."

Lesia laid a reassuring hand on her arm. "Rest. Sonia can rest with you. The land can wait. I've almost finished the third acre." She hesitated. "You are weak, Mama. Maybe even too weak to give birth. We need to get you strong. If I leave in the next few days, I'll be back by the end of July. With *food*! There's no other choice."

Mama's shoulders slumped. She looked defeated, beaten. She knew Lesia was right.

⁂

Andrew showed up the day before she had planned to leave. Lesia had just finished watering the garden when she heard the *clomp, clomp* of animal hooves on packed earth. A wagon pushed through the scrubby bush. Mama rushed outside, waving her arms excitedly in the air.

Lesia hurried over as Andrew jumped down from the wagon. He removed his hat and smiled. "Hello, Lesia."

She had forgotten how blue his eyes were. And what a warm smile he had. "Hello, Andrew."

Pearl was there, and so was Minnie, holding baby Mary and looking impossibly cool and well fed in a clean white blouse and pale green skirt. They must have been up before dawn to make the nineteen-mile trip. Lesia brushed the hair from her eyes and wished she'd had a chance to wash. Minnie always made her feel dirty.

"We came to check on you!" Pearl hoisted herself from the wagon and handed Mama a basket covered with a red-checkered towel. "There are a dozen eggs and cream, some pyrohy and fresh bread."

"How wonderful!" Mama clutched the basket to her chest. "Thank you."

Lesia's heart jumped. Now that they had food, maybe she wouldn't have to go out to work! Maybe Papa would return before the eggs ran out and she could stay and clear more land.

"You must see what we've done," Lesia said excitedly. "We have a garden and a root cellar and an oven. Mama and Sonia plastered the house and we've almost cleared—"

"Uncle Andrew," Minnie interrupted with a whine, "can you help me down?" She handed the baby to her mother.

"Of course."

Minnie reached for Andrew's hand before daintily alighting from the wagon. Trust Minnie, Lesia thought impatiently. Interrupting her when she was in the middle of good news. One of the oxen decided at that moment to shuffle his feet. Minnie wrinkled her nose in disgust as the dust floated into her face. Lesia hid her smile behind her hand.

"Where are Victoria and Anastasia?" Mama asked as Minnie rubbed vigorously at her face. "And Luka and Symon?"

"The twins would never sit still long enough for the trip," Pearl replied with a grin. "And the girls wanted to stay behind and go berry-picking."

Satisfied that her face was dust-free, Minnie stared at the dugout. "What is that?" she asked scornfully.

"Enough now," Pearl chided as she jiggled a suddenly fussy Mary. "You were born in a burdei just like that only days after we came to Canada." Holding the baby close, she followed Mama inside.

Andrew led the oxen to a patch of shade and went to get water. That left Lesia and Minnie alone.

Minnie's lip curled. "This is a dirt hovel, and the plaster job is terrible. Where's the fence? All *proper* houses have fences."

Lesia was stunned into silence. In the homeland, all Ukrainian houses did have fences. But this was Canada. And there were more important things than fences to tend to.

"You give the rest of us a bad name," Minnie continued in a low, mean voice. "Townsfolk talk about the poor, uneducated Ukrainians. 'Dirty continentals' they call us. That's you they're talking about. We're clean and rich. We have a fine house and acres of cultivated fields."

"Stop it!" Lesia wanted to reach out and smack the self-satisfied look from Minnie's face.

Minnie sneered. "You have nothing and you'll always have nothing. You should have stayed in the homeland. You'll never make it here."

"We've got three acres almost cleared!" Lesia retorted. "And I can read and write now, and some day we'll have animals too and a fancy house and—!"

"*Some* day." Minnie giggled and rolled her eyes skyward. "You know the rules. Thirty acres cleared in three years. You'll never make it." Andrew was coming. Minnie turned her back to him and whispered one last taunt—"Even with your big, fat muscles!"—and then she flounced away.

"Are you all right?" Andrew came to a sudden stop beside her.

"Fine." Lesia forced herself to smile. She was fine. She would be fine. Minnie was wrong.

"Come and walk with me," he said.

She led Andrew to the garden, chatting about the bug problem and how she was hand-picking three times a day to keep them under control. She showed him the bee skeps and said she was praying nightly for a colony of wild bees to settle.

After complimenting her on the size of her kale and the slim stalks of garlic greens, Andrew reached into his pocket and pulled out an envelope. "You said you could read in Ukrainian?"

Lesia's eyes flashed. "And write now too!"

"Good. This is for you."

There were a dizzying number of stamps on the envelope, and though the writing was in Ukrainian, it was heavily angled and hard to read. Lesia ripped it open and withdrew a single sheet of paper.

My dearest Lesia, Dmytro writes this for me as I ask. After explaining to Andrew that Dmytro was Baba's cousin, Lesia continued to read the letter out loud. *I must know—are you safe? Is Canada happy for you? Is Mama well? You can write now, yes? Please tell me the news of your land of milk and honey. Love, Baba.*

A lump of tears swelled in her throat. Lesia clutched the letter to her chest. How she missed dear Baba! She couldn't wait to put money away for her passage.

"Have you heard news of Papa?" she finally managed to ask Andrew. "Or Ivan?"

"Your father stayed on with the Icelandic fellow. Wasyl decided to go with Ivan and look for work in Winnipeg. The two of them stopped in on their way to town a few days ago." Andrew pulled a handful of bills from his pocket and held them out. "Your Papa sent this."

Baba's letter disappeared into her apron. Lesia took the bills and carefully counted them. Her eyes widened. Bozhe, she was holding thirty Canadian dollars.

Stunned, she looked up at Andrew. "This is worth seventy-five rynskys," she said breathlessly.

"Your father earned it over the last six weeks." Andrew fiddled with his hat. "Ivan gave it to me on behalf of Papa with . . . er . . . certain instructions."

Lesia's eyes narrowed. She knew her Papa all too well. "He told you to keep five dollars for Mama's doctor bill and give me the rest, didn't he?"

Two spots of bright pink flushed his cheeks. "Not . . . not exactly."

"Then what?"

"He told me to keep five dollars and spend the other twenty-five on supplies for you. But I didn't know what to buy so I thought I'd ask you first."

Carefully she counted off five one-dollar bills and held them out. "Here," she said.

Andrew took a step backward. "I won't take them."

"You must." She held her head proudly. "The Magus family pays its debts."

"You don't have to pay debts off all at once. That's why they call them debts." His eyes twinkled. "You have other debts to pay. You said so yourself. And your mama looks terrible. She needs to eat more potatoes."

Papa would kill her if she didn't pay Andrew. "You must take something."

"One dollar, then." He accepted the bill from Lesia's hand.

"Two." She shoved another at his fist.

"All right, two." He grinned. "Now what about the store?"

"The store?" But she wasn't really listening. *Twenty-eight dollars!* She could send twenty to Master Stryk, save a little for Baba's passage, maybe buy a bushel of potatoes or a sack of flour.

"Lesia?"

She snapped back. "I'll need to make a list," she said, "and think about how much to send to the master. I'll go to the store myself."

"The trail's rough in spots. It'll take you the better part of a day to walk to Hazelridge."

"It's summer. I can manage."

And Minnie said they'd never make it in Canada. The girl was crazy. Papa had already made it. She had twenty-eight Canadian dollars. Life was good!

Chapter Eight

Lesia settled herself near the small window near the corner of the burdei, reached for the family Bible and removed the pencil she'd hidden in its crease. Slowly, she pulled back the small square of muslin that covered the window and let the light from the full moon stream over the blank page.

Taking one of the cream sheets of paper Andrew had given her, Lesia laid it on top of the closed Bible and clutched the pencil between her fingers.

Dearest Baba, she wrote. *It is now July 23. Yes, we arrived safely. I am well. Mama and Sonia are well. Papa and Ivan are well. They have gone out to work.*

Sonia cried out softly in her sleep. Lesia's pencil skidded off the page. When the child had settled, Lesia resumed writing.

We have much land and a river filled with fish. Our house is very large with a great oven and many windows. We have two cows, six chickens and a hog. Soon we will have oxen and a plough. Canada is a special land. Its people are very kind. When you come, you will see. Your ever-loving Lesia.

By the time she was finished, the moon had moved and she was sitting in virtual darkness. But there was still one more letter to write.

She let herself outside quietly, being careful not to wake Mama and Sonia. Grateful for the moonlight and the orange glow that came from the dwindling fire, Lesia sat on a stump and balanced a second sheet of paper on the Bible.

Master Stryk Sir, she wrote, *I am sending you half of the money I borrowed. Soon I will send more.*

Somewhere, an owl hooted. Startled, Lesia jumped.

With a pounding heart, she turned back to her writing. *Canada is a rich country. There is much wood and food. Our land is vast. Our house is grand. We are rich and happy and free. Yours ever faithfully, Lesia Magus.*

She tucked both letters between the pages of the Bible and slipped back inside the burdei. Then she stretched out and shut her eyes. Tomorrow was a big day. She needed to sleep.

But sleep eluded her.

I should feel good, she thought. After all, she was sending Master Stryk fifty rynskys—twenty of her Canadian dollars. But Lesia didn't feel good at all.

She was a sinner.

For the first time in her life, she had lied before God. And to Baba, no less.

Bozhe! *Please understand. I cannot let Baba worry about us. I must convince her to leave Shuparka and come to Canada. I cannot allow the village to laugh at our foolish decision. I cannot allow Michal Stryk to laugh!*

Besides, Canada *was* the land of milk and honey. They *did* have lots of land. Papa had made thirty dollars! Soon they *would* have cows and chickens and hogs.

It was just a matter of time.

* * *

Lesia had been walking for over five hours towards the store in Hazelridge, stopping only for short rests in farmers' fields when she couldn't force herself to go on. She was tired, she was hungry, and her feet hurt. There was a small hole in the sole of her old boot. She could feel the dirt on the path rubbing against her skin and forming a blister. Still, she kept walking.

Michal Stryk was wrong. She *wasn't* useless or stupid or worthless. She wasn't rich yet, but she could walk into the store, hold her head high and proudly pay for whatever she wanted.

She'd mail the letters, buy flour and potatoes and oil. And she would buy a piglet or a colony of bees or maybe some chickens.

Up ahead, she could see a large grain elevator and some low, brown buildings. Hazelridge. Her heart began to pound.

It couldn't be as bad as Winnipeg. Could it?

She looked down at her clothes, the same clothes that had shamed her when she'd arrived months ago. They were dirty then. Now they were clean—or as clean as she could make them—but they were still full of holes. Still *different*.

She followed the rail line into town, looking nervously from left to right. There were buildings everywhere. The blacksmith was easy to spot, and so was the livery. But the store? It could be any building at all.

Then she saw it. The gathering place. Lesia counted three teams of horses and two pairs of oxen, all paired with wagons of various sizes, waiting outside. She slowed and watched as a man and a woman came down the steps and got into a large, fancy red wagon. An older man and a younger man wearing black overalls followed. Their arms were full of sacks and supplies. She could hear them as they loaded the wagon.

They were speaking English.

Her heart fell. She hesitated. Then she remembered Baba's words. *We are all worthy. We are all somebody.* She *was* worthy. She had taught herself to read and write, hadn't she? She had money, didn't she?

Lesia waited until the wagon had pulled away. Then, with her heart pounding, she followed the two men as they went back inside.

The store was large and crowded. People were talking all at once. German, English, Polish. The older man had taken his place behind a long counter, where he fetched and carried as people pointed to the goods on the shelves behind him. Lesia saw a sign with large, Ukrainian characters. It said "Jack Scott's General Store. If you cannot buy it here, you do not need it."

Andrew had told her the man was very British, but he had to be friendly if he had a Ukrainian sign. Perhaps this wouldn't be so hard, after all!

An older woman in a faded green apron showed three women a length of bright blue cotton. The plump young man in the overalls measured a wedge of butter on a large, shiny scale. A little girl with long black ringlets and big brown eyes ran back and forth behind the counter, from the young man to the older woman, and then back again. Pretty and petite, she couldn't be more than eight or nine. Lesia tried—and failed—to catch her eye. Instead, an old grey dog ambled up and licked her hand.

It was the only greeting she received.

She looked at the tables piled with tins of beans and jars of fancy jam. She studied the sacks under the table and marvelled at the oats and corn, grains of wheat and fat potatoes. She eyed the bolts of colourful fabric and the thick skeins of wool and wondered if she had enough money for either one. She waited patiently for the store to empty, but it never did. Instead, as one group left, others arrived.

Forcing her shyness aside, Lesia tried to catch the eye of the younger man. That didn't work. She moved closer to the older woman, but she paid no attention. It was the little girl who finally smiled and spoke, though in a language Lesia didn't understand.

Lesia smiled back. "Can you help me?" she asked in Ukrainian.

Giggling, the child fiddled with a shiny, silver scale. A large round of cheese slid close to the edge. Lesia lunged forward to grab it, knocking over a sack of beans in the process. The cheese fell with a smack, pinning the little girl's hand underneath. The girl screamed, and the woman in the faded green apron looked at Lesia as though she had thrown the cheese at the child. As the older man bent over to clean up, Lesia heard him say that horrible word she had come to recognize: *Bohunk.*

Lesia flushed. "I was trying to help," she said. They ignored her. She could hear drops of rain sleeting against the window. A storm was coming. She reached into the pocket of her apron, withdrew the cream sheets and waved them in the air. "I have letters to mail," she said shyly.

The man barked a reply. Lesia could feel all eyes studying her. Her stomach sank and her hands grew clammy. If she didn't make this man understand, the people in the store might laugh at her. Even worse, she might have to leave empty-handed.

"You wish to mail letters?" the younger man asked in a strange, halting mixture of Ukrainian and Polish. His round face was friendly; there was a trace of stubble on his chin. Thick brown hair kept falling into his eyes. Impatiently, he flicked it back.

"Yes, please!" He was being kind to her. And she could understand him! "Also, I would like to send money to the homeland." Her knees trembled with relief.

The young man frowned, pushed back his hair again and looked uncertainly at his father. The old man mumbled something under his breath.

She put twenty Canadian dollars on the counter. "I can pay."

The older man's eyes narrowed, but the younger man smiled and looked at his father for confirmation. The man studied Lesia with his cold, blue eyes. Finally, he shrugged his agreement.

Then everyone began talking again and the boy behind the counter became very busy. Lesia watched as her letters were stamped and filed. Politely, in his unusual mix of languages, the boy asked Lesia what else he could do for her. Politely, Lesia told him.

Was it money that made the difference? Or the decency of a stranger? Whatever it was, Lesia felt her confidence grow as her supplies were placed on the counter in front of her. A sack of flour, potatoes, some tea, a little sugar. Outside the sky remained dark. The rain continued to fall.

"Would you like a bolt of fabric?" the young man asked. "Or candles? Oil? Some candy?" He pointed to the baskets on the table.

She would love all of those things, Lesia thought, but she needed something that would produce food for the family. Shyly she asked to buy a colony of honey bees.

"None for sale," he said.

Lesia asked about the price of a cow.

"Forty-five dollars."

Her eyes widened. Papa would have to work for months before she could buy that! "What about piglets?"

"Seventy-five cents each. But we don't have any. Only three hogs. They're seven dollars each."

Lesia's shoulder's sagged. She stared at the goods on the counter. Perhaps she should put something back. But what? "How much are chickens?" she finally asked.

"Forty cents apiece."

Carefully she peered at the coins in her hand. Could she afford it?

"You could buy six." The young man answered her question before she could voice it.

But she wanted to put two Canadian dollars aside for Baba's passage. "I'll take two," Lesia said cautiously. As an afterthought she asked about the price of candy and oil. She could buy a little of both and still have some money left over.

Nervously she held out her hand and watched as the young man removed more coins. Then she carefully tucked the last of her money away.

"I'll get the chickens," he said. "Where's your cage?"

"Cage?"

"You do have a cage for them, don't you? Or a box?"

"No." Foolishly, she hadn't thought of that.

"What kind of wagon do you have?"

"I don't." She swallowed nervously.

The young man's eyes widened. "You're walking?"

Embarrassed, Lesia nodded. She could feel the older woman behind the counter studying her.

"Where do you live?"

She told him.

"That's hours away by foot."

"Yes."

"Longer in this weather." He ran a hand through his hair. "It's supposed to hail, you know."

He used an English word: *hail*. Lesia didn't know what that was. She agreed anyway.

She watched as he said something to his father. His father shook his head. The younger man sighed, gestured to Lesia and spoke again to his father. The older man frowned and answered sharply. Just like the weasel man who lived next door, Lesia thought. Not nice.

"Wait here." Then the young man was gone. Lesia tried to ignore the stares and whispers. The older woman was the worst; she looked sideways at Lesia and made *cluck*, *cluck*, *cluck*ing sounds with her tongue. And there were those words again. *Bohunk. Peasant scum.* Lesia wished the floor would open up and gobble her whole. She wished she'd never come to this town, this store. And for a fleeting minute, she wished she were back in Shuparka. She'd rather be dealing with Michal Stryk than this nastiness.

Finally the plump young man with the unruly hair was back, carrying a rectangular wooden box stamped with large, black letters. Lesia could hear the scratching of chicken feet against the bottom. "This box should hold the chickens," he said. "And I have a ride for you. Mr. Marchand is going within a mile or two of your farm." He handed her the box.

A ride! "Thank you!" Such kindness. And from a Canadian, no less. She peered inside the box. Two pairs of beady black eyes stared trustingly up at her. Lesia grinned.

"You'll have to walk the rest of the way, though." He studied the pile of goods on the counter with a skeptical frown. "Somehow," he added.

"I'll manage," Lesia said confidently.

She always managed somehow.

One of the chickens gave Lesia an encouraging squawk and she giggled under her breath. After all she'd been through, walking a few miles was nothing. Whether she had chickens and supplies or nothing at all. It was faith talking. Wouldn't Baba be proud!

Chapter Nine

August 1, 1914

The Magus homestead

Lesia's success in going to town and buying supplies gave her boundless energy. The Marchands had been kind enough to drive her all the way home, and because of their generosity, and Papa's earnings, she now felt hopeful and optimistic about the future. The chickens, aptly named Girlie and Noisy by Sonia, were laying more eggs than they could eat—three a day, sometimes four. Mama fried them in oil, boiled them for lunches and even baked paska, the rich egg bread they usually had at Easter.

Sonia's colds disappeared. Mama's face was rosy and full, and her bulging belly was a sign that the baby was growing well.

Lesia was up every day before dawn, letting the chickens out of the deep hole she'd dug to keep them safe at night, gathering the eggs and counting them. When she had enough, she would go to town and trade them for milk and a pickling crock.

Every day after egg collecting she watered the garden, checked the traps and stopped at the bee skeps, hoping to see even a quiet buzz of activity. Every day she would quell her disappointment and then head to the south field. In spite of the fact that the bees hadn't come, she was slowly but surely making progress on their land. The third acre was almost clear; soon she would start on the fourth. Ivan was right, the soil was hard and back-breaking, but Lesia was determined to tame it. Determined to break ten acres. Determined to prove Minnie wrong.

After dark, she would sit by the fire. When her eyes were too heavy for writing, she would work on her latest project, a woven willow fence for their property. The idea had come to her while she was weaving a cover for the chicken hole, but it was inspired by shame. When the Marchands had dropped her off a few weeks ago, they, like Minnie, had seemed to expect a landowner to have a fence.

The beet tops swayed lightly in the breeze as Lesia headed in for lunch one early August afternoon. She paused, admiring the swell of soil hinting at the red bulbs growing below the surface. Nearby, the beans were climbing their makeshift trellis, the small, tender vegetables hanging like baby fingers from the vines. Just a few more days and they'd be ready to pick!

If only Baba were here to see her garden overflowing with vegetables! To see the two chickens she had purchased with Papa's hard-earned money, and the fence she was building with her own hands. But Papa would see it. And so would Ivan. They would be so pleased!

"Lesia!" Mama called.

Looking up, she was surprised to see Andrew standing beside Mama and Sonia. She waved him over with a grin. "Soon we'll have beans to eat." She pointed proudly. "See them?"

"Yes." Andrew nodded.

"Andrew would like to spend some time alone with you." Mama gave her an encouraging look.

Lesia knew that Mama was thinking of a betrothal. She would like to have Andrew as a son-in-law. Not only was he caring, his land was productive, and he was good at saving money. But, while Andrew was hardworking and kind—two qualities she would want in a husband—Lesia couldn't think of such things while Papa was away.

Sonia tugged on Andrew's pant leg. "Andrei, Andrei!" Surprisingly, Andrew didn't pick her up and toss her into the air, as he often did. Instead, he held his hat in his hands and shifted awkwardly from one foot to the other. "I need to talk to you," he told Lesia. "Can we walk?" He gestured towards the creek.

"Of course." She had never seen Andrew look uncomfortable before. Her heart began to pound. What if did ask her to marry him? How would he feel when she had to say no? She fell into step beside him and they walked silently for several minutes.

"There is no easy way to tell you this." When they reached the edge of the creek, Andrew stopped. "I have another letter from the homeland. It is not good news."

Everything grew sharper then. The birds chirped more loudly, the wind rustled the leaves with greater intensity. The blood coursed through Lesia's veins, pounding in her ears. "What is it?" Uneasily she licked her lips. "What's happened?"

Andrew pulled two letters from behind his hat. "Here."

The paper was cool against her fingers, the tall, spiky Ukrainian writing familiar. Dmytro. One letter was addressed to Gregory and Ahafia Magus and family. The second was addressed to Lesia Magus. The postmark was Babyntsi, the nearest village to Shuparka. Lesia frowned as she stared at them. "How . . . how do you know they contain bad news?"

Pain flashed in Andrew's eyes. "I happened to be at the store when the mail arrived. Everything came in a package. The rest is in the wagon. There was a letter addressed to the postmaster. He opened it, and when he told me . . . well, I offered to take care of it."

"What . . . what is it?" Confused, she stared at Andrew. "What?"

His eyes were troubled but his voice was firm. "Open the letters, Lesia."

Her fingers fumbled with the letter addressed to her. Slowly she withdrew the slip of paper. She unfolded it carefully, and nervously she began to read.

Dear one, by the time you read this, I will be gone.

The words were Baba's. But where was she going? Puzzled, Lesia glanced up at Andrew. He was waiting, watching. She turned back to the letter.

Do not grieve for me. It is my time.

All of a sudden Lesia understood. She began to shiver uncontrollably. In spite of the warmth, she was viciously cold. "Baba?" she whispered. She shook her head from side to side. There was a terrible, vile taste in her mouth. "Not Baba." It was all wrong. There was a mistake. She waved the letter at Andrew. "No!" Her voice rose sharply. "Baba's coming here.

I'm saving for her passage. I need her here. She'll help me work the land. She'll help with the new baby. She'll teach me to make her healing medicines. She will do the mending. Baba's coming!"

The letter slipped out of Lesia's fingers and fell to the ground. She stared at the creek, where the water was down to a trickle because of the summer heat. "Baba's coming," she repeated thickly. "She's coming to see my creek. My garden."

Andrew retrieved the letter. "Sit down." He eased Lesia to the ground before sitting down beside her. "I'll read it to you."

Lesia leaned forward and rested her head on her knees. She felt nauseated, faint. It was wrong, all wrong. "No," she said weakly. "No, don't."

But Andrew wouldn't listen. He started from the beginning.

Dear one, by the time you read this, I will be gone. Do not grieve for me. It is my time. I am glad you are safe and well fed in Canada. I am glad you have many animals. Your life begins as my life ends. Let it be a joyful life. A prosperous life. Hold tight to your faith and remember, when you hold the Bible close, you hold me close. Because we are one in heart, I send to you the carved wooden box my baba gave to me. It is special, like Geebo's Bible. Mama will tell you about it. I love you, dear one. Hold your head up always. You are Lesia Magus. A proud Ukrainian. The heart of my heart. We are one. Forever, Baba.

Great gulping sobs shook her entire body. Andrew touched her hand in a gesture of comfort, but it made Lesia cry even harder. The only hand she wanted touching her now was Baba's. It could not be true. Bozhe, Bozhe! Baba was supposed to join them in Canada. She had two dollars set aside for her passage. They would all live together. What would she do now without dear Baba in her life?

Lesia wasn't sure how long she cried, but eventually her sobs lessened. Baba had died comforted by Lesia's lies. Was that good or bad? She didn't know.

Andrew spoke again. "There's another letter."

Lesia nodded. Of all the hardships they had endured since leaving Shuparka, none compared to the hardship of losing Baba. "Would you read it?" She wiped her eyes. "Please?"

Andrew opened the second envelope and withdrew a single sheet of paper.

To the Magus family, formerly of Shuparka, Galicia, he began. *I write on behalf of Nadia Chernetsky. She dictates this to me and will shortly dictate another letter to her beloved granddaughter, Lesia.* Andrew cleared his throat. *Dear ones, my cough worsens. I am old and it is time for my final journey. Do not mourn, for I will join our Heavenly Father and Geedo and Slavko. I will be a star to light your night sky. I have asked Master Stryk to send you a few rynskys for my land but the old man . . .* Andrew stopped suddenly.

Lesia looked at him. Andrew was staring at the paper. His lips quivered as he fought back a grin.

. . . the old man sometimes has hemp for brains and I do not know if he will remember.

Lesia giggled softly through her tears. Trust Baba!

I have asked Mary to lay me out. My body will rest with Geedo and Slavko. Already I have seen the white cross. It is very beautiful. Remember me at provody. My love will remain with you always. Baba.

"That's all?"

Andrew folded the letter. "Did you expect more?"

Lesia shrugged. Sunlight splashed through the trees and caressed her arms. The birds warbled sweetly. Life did indeed go on. Her life anyway.

"I don't know. It's just . . . there must be more to say when a life ends."

"No," Andrew replied softly. "Surprisingly little."

They exchanged glances. Lesia knew Andrew was thinking of his young wife. She knew he would understand when she said, "I loved her desperately."

His eyes were sad. "I know." He reached for her hand, and this time Lesia allowed him to take it.

"With her I could be myself," Lesia murmured. "I could be silly or sad or afraid. It didn't matter. She believed in me like no one else." Who would take Baba's place? Who could? No one.

Grief, thick and heavy, settled on Lesia's heart. "I'll never forget her," she told Andrew softly. "Never!"

He squeezed her hand. "I'm sure you won't."

"Will you help me tell Mama and Sonia?"

"Of course." He pulled her to her feet and together they walked slowly back to the burdei.

Chapter Ten

"I remember when we were young she would bring it out on special occasions and tell us about her Geedo, who had spent years working on it." It was evening now, and Mama spoke softly, in order not to wake Sonia. Her fingers caressed the delicately carved box before she handed it to Lesia.

The detail was exquisite. Even in the pale glow from the candlewick burning in oil, the gleaming wood was a rich nut brown. Lesia's fingers traced flowers and bees, which represented the sweetness of life, and a perfectly round sun, which represented Lada, the Ukrainian goddess of love and life. It was the most beautiful thing she had ever owned. But it would never take the place of Baba.

"Ooh!" Mama rubbed her stomach.

"Are you all right?" Lesia asked nervously.

"Just a twitch," she said.

Mama had taken the news of Baba's death calmly, but her face had drained of colour instantly and she had remained pale all day. Now, with Sonia in bed for the night, she seemed more grief-stricken than ever.

"It's hard seeing this." Hands trembling, Mama held up Baba's hairbrush. "And this." She reached for Baba's treasured scissors. They'd been a gift after Baba had attended the difficult birth of a baby born to a rich woman who lived several villages away.

They were going through the larger wooden crate Andrew had pulled from his wagon before he'd left. Lesia, like Mama, was overcome with memories. There were a few cooking utensils and the heavy can Baba had used to carry water from the well. Lesia's eyes filled with tears. She could almost see Baba coming through the door complaining that it grew heavier every day. There were colourful skeins of wool and a half-finished woven belt. Baba's last project. She would finish it in her memory, Lesia vowed. And maybe make another one. There were more blankets. Another shawl. Baba's thick black skirt and the fancy sorochka she wore to church.

"They must have buried her in her summer clothes," Lesia murmured absently. Her hands fastened around a large jar of honey. She smiled. That wasn't Baba's. Someone in the village had included it as a gesture of hope and kindness.

"Ooooooh." Mama clutched her stomach and bent forward.

"What is it, Mama?" Lesia demanded sharply.

"The baby." Mama's voice was thick with pain. "I think it's time."

"Now, Mama?" Fear swept down Lesia's back. The shock of Baba's death was bringing on the baby. It was only August 10; the baby wasn't due until sometime in September. "It's too early!"

Mama was overcome with another spasm. "Babies come when they want to, not when we think they should," she finally gasped. "Besides, it's not that early. Three weeks. Maybe a month."

"But . . . but . . . I . . ." Lesia trembled. She'd never delivered a baby before. Baba had always been the one. *Oh, Baba!* Lesia fought back tears and stared wildly around the tiny burdei. Where could she put Mama? How could she keep Sonia from waking? What if . . . what if it didn't go well? What if the baby wasn't healthy?

So many questions. And no answers.

"Mama, Andrew will be back tomorrow. Remember? After he takes the eggs to town, he'll be back with milk. Hold on till then!" She didn't know what Andrew could do, but his presence would be a comfort.

Mama's laugh turned into a garbled moan. "Lesia, it does me no good to hold on. This baby is coming."

"I'll run and tie a white cloth to the fence. Someone is bound to stop." No one on the prairie would ignore the universal cry for help.

"There's no time. We need to prepare." Mama straightened, moved slowly to the corner, lowered herself to a blanket and started giving her instructions.

Lesia followed them quickly and carefully. She built up the outside fire, filled Baba's can with water and put it on to boil. She lined their clean wooden box with hay and a clean blanket. Mama asked for string but they had only thread. Near the thread went oil and flour and another blanket. She tucked Baba's scissors in her apron pocket. On impulse, Lesia added Baba's shawl to the pile.

"What are these things for, Mama?" Lesia asked.

But Mama couldn't answer. "OOOoooooooh," she groaned.

"Mama?" Sonia sat up and groggily rubbed at her eyes. "Mama?"

"It's all right, little one. Mama's baby will be coming soon. Sleep now," Lesia urged reassuringly. "Sleep."

"Outside," Mama whispered. "I need to be outside so Sonia can sleep."

"No, Mama!" Lesia was horrified at the suggestion. "We don't know what's out there. Coyotes, skunks. Besides, the ground is dirty. You can't have the baby outside."

"I have to!"

Sonia sat up and began to cry. "Maaama!"

"Help me up, Lesia." Mama's eyes were sharp with pain. "Now!"

Lesia did it. Mama tottered on her feet and clutched at Lesia's arm before moving to the door. "Don't worry . . . about . . . noise," she whispered. "Always . . . noise." She drew a ragged breath. "Ohhhh." Mama doubled over and stuffed her fist into her mouth to smother another cry. She squeezed Lesia's arm so hard it made her wince.

"Mama!" Sonia jumped up. "Mama sick?" she asked uncertainly, coming to stand behind them.

"Hush, little one." Lesia attempted a reassuring smile. "Mama will be fine. Go back to bed now."

Lesia knew the pain had lessened when Mama eased her grip on her arm. She straightened and whispered again. "Tend Sonia. Wait until she's asleep. Then come down to the garden. Bring everything." She let go of Lesia's arm and slowly waddled through the door, one hand bent backwards, rubbing at the base of her spine.

"Mama!" Sonia would have hurled herself out the door if Lesia hadn't stopped her.

"Everything is fine, darling." Firmly she guided her sister back to bed, eased her down and tucked the blanket around her. "Soon you will have a new sister or brother." Lesia stretched out beside Sonia and pulled her close. Only then did she shut her eyes for a quick, silent prayer. *God willing.*

The words caught the child's attention. "The boy kind." Her breath was soft and sweet on Lesia's chin.

She smiled. "That's a brother."

"A brother." Sonia yawned. "Night, Lessie."

"Sleep well." She planted a kiss on her sister's downy head.

Lesia wanted Sonia to go to sleep right away—and she wanted her to stay awake all night. She wanted to help Mama, and yet she didn't. What was it that Baba used to say? That birth and death are two sides of the same coin. The memory of Baba stabbed at Lesia's heart, and she could feel tears gathering behind her eyes. Furiously she blinked them away. Baba wouldn't want her to cry. Not now.

Soon Sonia's breathing slipped into a regular rhythm. Slowly Lesia eased her arm away and peered at her sister. She was sleeping peacefully. Hopefully she would stay that way until morning.

Grabbing the makeshift cradle and supplies, Lesia stepped

outside. The night was clear, the sky was full of stars. The fire crackled and burned, sending sparks into the darkness. The water in Baba's carrying can hissed and bubbled. Could she carry it and the cradle too?

No. She would have to make two trips.

She moved swiftly towards the garden, quickly adjusting to the sounds of night. The low hoot of an owl. The snap of her feet on a twig as she followed the familiar path.

Then she heard another sound—a low moan that quickly turned into a wail.

"I'm coming, Mama!" She clutched her supplies and began to run.

The wail crested and dropped. Another low moan took its place. Lesia followed the sound and found Mama at the end of the garden, near the corn.

"I'm here now." Lesia dropped to her knees and cradled Mama's face between her hands.

"Lesia." Mama's eyes were shut but she smiled weakly. "So glad . . . the baby . . . is coming."

Bozhe, not already! "Mama, I have to get the water. We need hot water, remember?"

Mama's eyes opened. She attempted a nod. "Go now."

Lesia ran back to the fire, yanked off her apron, wrapped it around and around the handle of the old tin can and hurried back.

"Baba was right," she panted, placing it on the ground nearby. "This old can just gets heavier and heavier."

But Mama didn't hear. Her eyes were shut; she was moaning, low and deep. Her hair was slick with sweat and plastered to her head. Her face glowed a sickly white in the darkness.

"I . . . must . . . push." Mama struggled to sit up.

There was a lump the size of a plum in Lesia's throat. Bozhe! According to Baba, the pushing could go very fast or very slow. Either way, beloved Baba had always been so solemn when she talked about the pushing part. It was, she had said, the most dangerous part of all.

Lesia swallowed but the lump in her throat wouldn't go away. "Now, Mama?"

"Up." Mama leaned on her elbow. "Stand up . . . to . . . push."

In spite of her massive stomach, Mama was still thin. Lesia, on the other hand, was stronger and more muscular than she'd ever been. It was no trouble to cradle Mama as she squatted in the garden.

Mama was so quiet at first Lesia thought she'd fallen asleep. But then she felt it. Mama's body tensing. Her belly shaking. A deep groan rumbled into the darkness. Lesia tightened her arms while Mama pushed.

Nothing.

Three times that happened. Mama tensed and groaned and pushed. And nothing happened.

The fourth time was different.

This time, the noise came first. And this noise was like no other. It was a loud, powerful howl that sent shivers down Lesia's spine.

"Nooooooowwwwwwwww!" Mama leaned forward. Her face contorted as she struggled to release the baby she had carried to this new land.

"Nooooooowwwwwww," she moaned again. Her body

tightened and she pushed. Lesia could feel a shift in energy. Movement.

Mama fell back.

Lesia's eyes widened. "The baby!" she breathed. "Mama, the baby is half out."

Mama's eyes were closed but her body was tensing again. Another guttural moan was coming.

"Push, Mama," Lesia urged. "Push!"

And Mama did.

The baby slipped into Lesia's hands. Shocked, she could only stare. It was a baby. Fresh and newborn. Covered in bits of blood and white slop and still attached by its silvery blue cord to Mama. And it was a boy! Just like Sonia wanted.

Upside down! Lesia could hear Baba's voice. *Turn him upside down.*

Lesia turned him. He sputtered and coughed. And then he began to wail softly.

His mouth. She could hear Baba again. *Clear his mouth.*

"Baby?" Mama said weakly. "See . . . the . . . baby."

His mouth! She wasn't sure if she was imagining the words or really hearing them, but she turned her little brother over. He was as slippery as a fresh fish. With her index finger, she reached as far into his mouth as she dared. Mucus was clogging his throat. As soon as she removed it, the baby's wail grew stronger, more forceful. *Ach, yes . . .* And Baba's voice gently faded away.

"Baby," Mama reached for him.

Lesia put her brother into Mama's arms. "It's a boy," she said softly.

Mama stared down at her newest child. "A blanket," she whispered. "We must cover him."

Wordlessly, Lesia tucked it around the baby, being careful not to touch the cord. She would not look at that. It seemed to be pulsating and moving. Instead, she stared at her little brother. His eyes were open, watchful, unblinking. She grinned. He was so peaceful, so accepting.

Did he look like Slavko? Lesia wondered. She didn't remember Slavko as a baby. She'd been young herself when he was born. But she had been old enough to remember everything when he died.

Mama glowed with happiness as she examined his tiny fingers, traced the dark lines of his brows. "Your Papa will be so proud," she whispered. "Of him and of you."

"But Mama, I did nothing." Now that it was all over, Lesia felt her part *was* nothing.

"Ah!" Mama smiled. "But there's more to do. Remember the thread? And the oil? And the flour?"

Lesia nodded.

"The thread is to tie off the cord. You'll have to do that and cut it, too. Then we'll clean him and dust him and swaddle him."

"But—"

Mama reached out and touched Lesia's lips with her finger. "Hush. You can do it, moye sonechko. There's nothing to be frightened of now. The worst is over." She turned back to the baby.

Pushing is the most dangerous part of all.

The voice was so clear and so strong that Lesia whirled around, expecting to see Baba standing behind her. *Dearest*

Baba, Lesia thought, *I learn of your death on the day God gives me the gift of a baby brother!*

Following Mama's instructions, Lesia sterilized Baba's scissors and pulled the thread around and around the cord. After it was cut, she cleaned the infant and gently rubbed oil into the creases of his arms and legs while Mama delivered the afterbirth. Carefully Lesia took some flour and dusted the bit of cord that was still attached to his stomach. Soon, Mama told her, it would turn black and fall off. Finally it was time to wrap the baby and put him in the cradle.

"Not a blanket, Mama. This." Lesia reached for Baba's shawl.

"Yes." Mama's smile was tinged with sadness.

Lovingly, Lesia wrapped her little brother in the warmth of the colourful shawl and then placed him in the cradle. She tucked another blanket securely around him.

"We will call him Adam," Mama said. Her eyes were shut. She looked peaceful.

Adam had been Geedo's name. Awestruck, Lesia studied his perfectly shaped eyebrows, his thick lashes, his small, pink hands. For a long while, he studied her back, silent yet alert. Eventually, his eyes grew heavy and he drifted off to sleep.

Soon she would have to help Mama and Adam back to the burdei. But for a minute, she just wanted to enjoy the peacefulness of the night.

The dark sky was huge, like an upturned bowl of velvet, glittering and shimmering with stars. As she watched, a star shot in a silver arc over her head before disappearing over the edge of the horizon.

Lesia smiled. She felt blessed.

Chapter Eleven

Ah, my darling Laisha, I never forgot Baba. My grief for her was like a shirt that I wore until it crumbled into dust and became part of my skin.

Adam helped. He cried on and on in those early weeks. Then, he grew into such a happy, loving baby. He was a joy to care for. When we had eggs to trade for milk and butter, and when we still had flour and potatoes, Adam grew plump on the richness of Mama's milk.

I would stare in awe. Adam was a promise fulfilled. A rich reward from the land of milk and honey. A blessing from God. For the first time ever, Mama was able to nurse a baby quiet. Fill a belly. I was so proud. So hopeful.

I worked hard, always so hard, but especially those weeks after Adam's birth. There was Sonia to care for and meals to cook and still the land to clear and the fence to weave. Mama could not help. She was too weak to do more than nurse Adam, so it was all left to me. Some nights I fell asleep in my chair. But it was worth it. All of it.

God took Baba, yes, but He gave us Adam to ease our pain. In His infinite wisdom, God knew what was best. So Baba had always said. I had my grief, but this I accepted.

When the horror came, I was able to see that Baba's passing was a blessing too. She was old already. She had known misery. She did not need to live with more.

Ah, my darling Laisha, the shame of that time. Bozhe! Bozhe! The fear and the anger and the styd. How you say that in English? The disgrace. Baba would have died a thousand deaths to learn of it.

It was better that she was gone. I could take comfort at night when the stars winked down at us. She was there, sending us light in all the darkness.

For some things that happened under that prairie sky are so horrible they are without words. Unspeakable. Unacceptable. Then and now.

September 5, 1914

The Magus homestead

The evening was still and warm and the mosquitoes loved it. They swarmed at Lesia, biting whatever skin was exposed—her hands, her feet, her face. With a cry of anger, she slapped her neck, flicked another dead insect to the ground and rubbed her blood-smeared hand down the side of her apron. If she could resist the urge to scratch, the bites would stop itching soon enough.

Raising the axe above her head, she let her anger and frustration propel it down onto another tree stump. She wanted honey in the hives, wheat in the fields and respect in the eyes of the townspeople.

Instead, the hives were empty, there were acres left to clear and the respect she had come to Canada to find had eluded her.

Zzzzzzzz. She dropped her axe and swatted her ear. Another mosquito fell to the ground. Wearily, she surveyed the land. Three acres clear, seven more to go. She hadn't gotten far tonight, but at least it was something.

If only they had land without tree stumps and scrub! If only they had soil that crumbled like breadcrumbs. If only they had wheat already planted.

A mosquito flew into her eye. Another attacked her nose. With a cry of disgust, Lesia grabbed her axe and headed for the smoky fire burning outside the burdei. Twilight was fading; soon it would be dark.

The sight of tall poppies laden with full, ripening pods lifted her spirits as she walked past the garden. The sunflowers had blossomed and set seed too. Soon it would be time to harvest both and turn them into oil.

A mosquito bit her hand. Several more were stinging her ears. Enough! She started to run.

A thin, stooped man was standing in front of the burdei, a shotgun resting over one shoulder and a flat brown package on the other.

"Papa!" The axe went flying. The mosquitoes and all her worries were forgotten. She ran forward and flung herself into his arms.

He wrapped her in a bear hug. "For a minute, I thought I was in the wrong place. There is the start of a fence near the road. Curtains on the window. I even thought I heard chickens."

Lesia laughed and pulled back. "You did, Papa. We have chickens now. I bought them with the money you sent. And the garden is growing, and I've cleared another acre."

Papa lowered the shotgun and the package to the ground. The corners of his moustache curved into a half smile. "Well done, moye sonechko." He was smaller than she remembered. And he looked tired; his face was deeply lined.

"Gregory?" Mama pushed aside the fabric that covered the door. Stunned surprise replaced the uncertainty on her face. "Oh, Gregory. It really is you! And I thought I was dreaming." She disappeared from sight, reappearing a few seconds later with a blanketed bundle in her arms.

"Meet your son," she said with a brilliant smile. "Adam."

"A son!" The news energized Papa. He threw his shoulders back and raised his hands to the sky in gratitude. "Thanks be to God," he shouted. "A boy."

"Hush, you'll wake him! And Sonia." Mama giggled and handed Adam over. "Besides, you should thank Lesia, she's the one who helped him into the world."

Gently, Papa peeled back the blanket to get a closer look. Lesia peered over his shoulder, still amazed at the lovely creases of fat that were starting to appear on the baby's tiny legs.

"Plump," Papa murmured in disbelief. "Fat almost. How old?"

"Almost a month," Mama whispered back.

He and Mama stared at each other. "My son," Papa said in awe.

"Yes," Mama replied.

Lesia knew they were both thinking of Slavko.

They settled on log stumps by the fire, where Lesia broke the news about Baba. Papa raised his eyes to the now-dark sky and said, "God gave with one hand and took with the other." Grief-stricken, he hugged Adam to his chest and rocked back and forth. "Will the trouble never end?" he murmured. His shoulders shook in mute testimony to his grief.

Lesia and Mama exchanged nervous glances. "What trouble?" Lesia asked.

But Papa didn't answer. Instead, he continued to rock, continued to mutter about Adam and Baba and the ironies of the world. Finally calm, he handed Adam back to Mama, wiped the tears from his eyes and leaned forward onto his knees. "War has been declared in the homeland," he said, his voice suddenly gruff. "And Canada is involved."

Mama gasped.

Lesia stiffened. Her first thought was of Baba. But Baba was in God's hands and out of harm's way. "Ivan and I were right, then. We left just in time."

"Perhaps yes. Perhaps no." Papa shrugged. "You see, little one, Galicia belongs to Austria. We are Austrian in the eyes of the world. And Canada is at war with Austria."

Sap from a piece of wood hit the fire with a crack. Lesia jumped. "But we're Ukrainian," she said uneasily.

"The Canadian government doesn't see the difference," Papa told her.

"What does that mean?"

The frown between Papa's eyes deepened into a slash of

worry. "At best, nothing. At worst, they will watch us carefully and make sure we aren't politically involved."

"What about Ivan?" Mama looked stricken.

Lesia cringed. Keeping her brother out of politics was like trying to keep Sonia still—almost impossible.

"He's still in Winnipeg. Somewhere. Pray for him," Papa added quietly.

After a long minute of silence, Mama spoke. "I see you bought a gun." She gestured to the brown package beside it. "But what's that?"

Brightening, Papa jumped up and retrieved his purchases. "I bought a window to keep out the winter cold. The gun so we can hunt through the winter. And new boots." He pointed to his feet, clearly proud of his practicality. "They say in winter the snow is so deep and cold it can freeze your toes in minutes. These will keep us warm when we hunt. We can share them."

What good were new boots when they had no food?! Their old boots might be falling apart, but they could mend them like they mended their clothes.

"Papa, bugs are overtaking the garden. Some of our potatoes are growing stunted because the soil is so poor. We have eggs now, but the chickens won't lay in winter. We need more food. An indoor stove. Oxen to help clear the land. A cow for cream and butter." Lesia took a breath. *Respect from the townspeople.* "We made a vow, Papa, that no one in the Magus family would go hungry again, remember?"

"We'll manage," Papa reassured her. "But debts must be cleared, Lesia. I just mailed fifty rynskys to Master Stryk and—

"But I sent him fifty rynskys too."

"Good!" Papa said proudly. "Then that debt is clear." He paused and stroked his moustache. "You managed very well on just five dollars, Lesia."

She flushed. Papa had done some quick addition in his head. If Andrew had kept the money they owed him, Lesia would have had just five dollars left from the thirty Papa had earned. "Andrew wouldn't take the money," she admitted. "Not all of it. He wanted to take only a dollar, but I insisted he take two. I still have two dollars set aside for Baba's passage."

"That can go to Andrew. We must pay him back. The Magus family will not be indebted to anyone." Though his body looked beaten and his face was weathered and tired, Papa's eyes still burned with the strength of his convictions.

Frustration made Lesia rash. "We must take care of ourselves first, Papa. We must feed ourselves and make some money. We want to hold our head up high in this new land. We want—"

"I did what I thought was best," Papa interrupted angrily. "You bought flour and oil and chickens. And I bought a rifle and a window and boots. Together, we paid down our debt. Now it's time to get back to clearing the land. And we must work fast, Lesia. There's no telling what the coming months will bring."

Chapter Twelve

September 20, 1914

The Magus homestead

At first, the war didn't affect Lesia and her family. Their life quickly slipped into a productive routine.

Mama gathered eggs, wove the fence, tended the garden and the children and cooked meals. Lesia and Papa dug and pulled and cleared. Though Papa had lost weight, he was still strong. Between them, they accomplished the work of three powerful men. Lesia's muscles screamed with fatigue, but the sight of the fourth acre being cleared fuelled her. It also helped that the intense heat of summer had been replaced by cooler, shorter days.

As she worked on Baba's belt by candlelight, Lesia wondered about Ivan. From the whispers between Mama and Papa, she knew they were wondering too. But the work kept her mind and hands occupied, and when the first belt was finished, she started a second one.

The weather grew colder and still there was no sign of Ivan. In the morning, Lesia's skin was covered in gooseflesh and her words came out in puffs of white. The distant fields were golden brown and if she stared hard she could see small moving figures bringing in the harvest. On their own homestead, she and Mama had pulled sixty heads of garlic and gathered two sacks of poppy seeds and sunflower seeds.

Andrew had promised to take her to the Boychuk farm in Oakbank, where there was an oil press, but, like Ivan, he was nowhere to be found. He'd visited twice the week after Adam was born, but then his visits had stopped.

"It's harvest time," Papa reminded her. "Not only that, he's a Canadian citizen. He may have enlisted."

Enlisted? How strange to think that if they'd stayed in Shuparka, Andrew might have been fighting against them. The whole idea of war frightened her.

Instead of Ivan or Andrew, Lesia was surprised to see an official on horseback ride into the clearing one cloudy morning. In spite of Mama's warning that she could smell rain in the air, Lesia was outside hanging Adam's blanket, while Sonia played on the ground nearby.

"Are you the lady of the house?" The man wore a scarlet jacket, black trousers and a wide-brimmed beige hat. A Mountie! Lesia had heard all about the men who kept law and order in Canada. Why was he here?

"The lady of the house?" He said it a second time, and when Lesia didn't answer, he tried "Lady or man of the house?" in halting Ukrainian and stared down his nose like she was a speck of dirt on his shiny black boots.

"Mama," she yelled over her shoulder. "Come quick."

When Mama caught sight of the Mountie, she thrust Adam into Lesia's arms and mumbled, "I'll get Papa." Scooping Sonia up, she hurried off to the field where Papa worked.

The man dismounted, grabbed the reins and tethered his horse to a nearby tree. Lesia turned back to her washing. It was impossible to do anything while she held Adam, but she wasn't going to just stand there staring.

"Yes?" Papa's voice thundered confidently through the clearing.

The Mountie strode forward. He was more than a head taller than Papa. Heavier too. But Lesia was proud to see that Papa didn't flinch.

"I'm travelling through the district checking citizenship papers," the man said in English. "A matter of procedure."

"They are inside." Papa turned to the burdei. "I will get them."

Lesia smothered a gasp. When had Papa learned English? She couldn't understand the words, but she had recognized English since that trip to the store. Adam squirmed in her arms and she handed him back to Mama, who was staring after Papa with a curious look on her face. Obviously she was just as surprised.

"Here." Papa returned and thrust their documents at the Mountie.

The man studied them for several minutes before looking up. "There are four papers here, but there are five of you."

Papa looked proud as he pointed to the baby. "My son Adam is a Canadian citizen. He was born here six weeks ago."

At the mention of Adam's name, Mama looked terrified. She clutched the baby with one hand and held Sonia against her leg with the other. Lesia gave her a reassuring smile. Papa was calm. Surely there was nothing wrong.

"Are there others?"

"My older son, Ivan," Papa said. "He's in Winnipeg."

Lesia held her breath. She studied the Mountie carefully. She'd become skilled at understanding body language and facial expressions. He didn't seem interested in Ivan.

"You are Austrian, are you not?" he asked.

Lesia's heart thumped. She expelled her breath and shot Mama a worried glance. Austrian was a word they both recognized. It was a word they had come to fear.

"We are Ukrainians," Papa said proudly. "From Shuparka."

"Shuparka?" The man frowned. "Where is Shuparka?"

"In Galicia, Ukraine," Papa replied.

"Ah." A self-righteous smile touched the Mountie's lips. "You are Austrian then." He waved the papers in the air.

"We are Ukrainians," Papa said quietly. "From Ukraine."

The Mountie ignored him. "On orders from the Canadian government and under the War Measures Act, you must register as an enemy alien. Do you understand?"

"Yes." Papa nodded.

"You must also report to a government official every month."

Papa seemed to shrink before Lesia's very eyes. "Yes."

"Once you register, you must stay on this farm. You cannot leave for any reason. Do you understand?"

"Yes."

Adam began to cry. Mama shushed him. Lesia's heart hammered against her chest. Her earlier confidence wavered. She couldn't understand the words, but she knew something wasn't right.

"Furthermore," the Mountie continued, "you are reminded of your agreement with my government. You must cultivate thirty acres in the next three years or the land will be taken away. You must pay your taxes yearly or also face losing the land."

Papa was silent. Lesia and Mama exchanged glances.

The Mountie waited for an answer. "Do you understand?"

Papa was still silent.

"Sir?"

Speak, Papa, speak, Lesia wanted to scream. But her lips refused to move.

"I understand," Papa finally said.

Satisfied, the Mountie handed the papers to Papa and turned towards his horse.

The sight of the man's back seemed to infuriate Papa. "Why are you doing this?" he demanded angrily. "Why? We have done nothing to hurt you. To hurt Canada. Why bother us?"

The Mountie turned back. Lesia was surprised to see traces of compassion in the man's blue eyes. "Just carrying out orders, sir. All enemy aliens must register. I've been ordered to find them, that's all." The Mountie untethered his horse and tipped his hat. "Good day."

Silently they watched him disappear from view.

"What did he say?" Lesia demanded. "Why are you upset?"

It didn't take Papa long to recap the conversation.

"Register as enemy aliens?" Lesia was shocked. "And report to the government? But why?"

"I told you when I came home. They think we're Austrians," Papa said.

"That's ridiculous," Lesia said flatly.

"Of course it is. I'm no enemy alien. But they'll think what they want to think." Papa stared into space, considering.

"We aren't enemies of Canada and we shouldn't be forced to call ourselves that." There was a proud, patriotic tilt to Mama's chin. "For years, we let the government dictate to us at home. And look what happened. We lost our land, our livelihood, our son." Her voice trembled at the mention of Slavko. "We cannot let it happen again."

"This isn't Galicia," Lesia reminded Mama. "This is Canada. Remember what Ivan said. It's a democracy here."

Papa sighed. "But there are laws, and we have to follow them. I'll go to Winnipeg and register. I'll find Ivan and bring him home. I'll sell the eggs, too. We need shells for the shotgun and more potatoes. If need be, I'll use Lesia's two dollars. Andrew will have to wait. The war may be over tomorrow, but the winter will be long and cold. We have to be prepared."

"I'll take the seeds and walk with you as far as Cooks Creek," Lesia said. "Then I'll turn off to Andrew's farm."

"Paul's farm is miles before Andrew's," Mama reminded her. "Go straight to the Korols. They'll know where to get the seeds pressed."

Mama was right. Lesia nodded.

"We'll leave in the morning," Papa told her.

"God be with you," Mama murmured softly. "Both of you."

* * *

When they reached Cooks Creek, where Papa would head west for Winnipeg and she would go east, Lesia was suddenly overcome with emotion.

"I love you, Papa," she whispered in his ear, fiercely blinking back tears. All this talk of war and enemy aliens had sickened her. Saying goodbye to Papa now left her breathless with fear. "Hurry back to Mama."

With one final hug, Papa handed her the second sack of seeds and was gone.

Lesia couldn't walk very fast. She had two seed bundles on her shoulders and her boots were falling apart. In spite of her best efforts to mend them, they were little more than scraps of leather held together by bits of twine.

Papa may have been foolish to insist on paying Master Stryk back so quickly, Lesia thought with a wince as she caught a pebble between her toes, but perhaps buying new boots wasn't such a bad idea. Papa had wanted her to wear them, but she had insisted he keep them. It was only fair. He had thirty miles to cover. She had only nineteen.

By the time Lesia caught sight of the Korols' farm, it was early evening. Her feet were bloodied and her eyes were swollen with exhaustion. Adam's fussing had prevented her from getting a good night's sleep and they had started their journey before dawn.

Turning into the gate, she saw wagons. Lots of them. The Korols had company.

She stared at her feet. Everyone would see her like this. There would be questions about her, about Papa. She couldn't tell them about the Mountie. She was too ashamed.

A burst of laughter floated into the air, followed by the pungent smell of roasted meat. Bozhe, she was hungry.

So what if everyone stared? So what if they asked questions? She just wouldn't answer. She knocked on the front door and waited.

Andrew answered.

Lesia's knees trembled. A relieved smile flitted over her face. "You're here."

"Everybody's here." He took the sacks from her aching arms. "The harvest is finished. Finally."

"I brought my seeds to be pressed."

He grinned and ushered her inside. "I was hoping you didn't walk all this way for nothing."

Maybe it was hunger or maybe it was fatigue, but everything passed in a blur after that. Smiling strangers touched her arms and stroked her hair. Pearl pressed a plate of food into her hand while Paul removed her boots and carefully bathed her feet. The only questions came from Andrew, but Pearl shushed him, and, after a second helping of food, Lesia was given a bed in the back room, where she promptly fell into a deep sleep.

When she woke the next morning, her belly was still full, her feet were covered in Pearl's homemade liniment, and the strange wagons in the Korols' yard were gone.

After breakfast, the older woman packed a basket of food to accompany her and Andrew to the pressman's farm.

"Andrew will be right here." Efficiently, Pearl settled Lesia in the wagon and tucked the sacks of seeds behind her. "I just wish Paul would spend more time on farming and less time on politics." With a vigorous flick of her wrist she shook out a coarse brown blanket, draped it over Lesia's knees and tucked it in. "I hate all this talk of war."

"Me too," Lesia admitted quietly. She could see Minnie approaching and she didn't want the girl to hear. She kept her head bent and pretended to study the repairs Paul had made to her boots. "Perhaps it will be over soon."

"One can hope." Pearl frowned and stared into the distance. But then her gloomy mood lifted and she smiled. "Here's Minnie to keep you company until Andrew comes. Say hi to your Mama for me. And give little Adam a hug."

Lesia stared longingly after Pearl. She did not want to be left alone with Minnie! *Hurry up, Andrew!*

"Had any visitors lately?" Minnie asked smugly.

Lesia was silent. She could see Andrew and Paul walking slowly towards the wagon. *Hurry up!*

"We did," the girl continued. "A Mountie."

Lesia stared silently ahead. Out of the corner of her eye, she could see a nasty little grin on Minnie's narrow mouth.

"I told him about you."

Involuntarily, her head jerked towards Minnie. "You what?"

If Minnie was taken aback by the coldness in Lesia's voice, she didn't show it. "Enemies of the state. That's what you are. I heard him ask Papa. Papa said nothing. But later, when the Mountie was leaving, I told him about you," she said with a satisfied smirk. "And where you lived."

Lesia's stomach knotted together in anger and disgust. It was all Minnie's fault that Papa had to report to the police. She'd known the girl was nasty, but vicious behaviour like this was incomprehensible. Ignoring the fury that rolled through her like water coming to a boil, Lesia forced one word through clenched teeth. "Why?"

"You're not a Canadian." Minnie kept one eye on the approaching men. "And you're not Ukrainian either. People from Galicia are Austrians." She spat out the word as if it were a piece of food gone bad. "I told you before, you're not one of us. Not with rags for clothes and scraps for boots. Not with your little hut on that piece of wilderness you call a farm."

"So," Paul boomed as he approached them, "did Pearl bring out the basket of food?"

"Yes, Papa," Minnie said sweetly as she tucked her hand through her father's arm. "I helped Mama pack it myself."

How *dare* she pretend nothing was wrong? Cold revulsion gave Lesia strength. She'd had enough of this!

Andrew climbed in beside Lesia. "Ready?" he asked.

"Almost." She leaned forward and looked Paul straight in the eye. "I'm surprised your daughter would help a Galician," she said bluntly. "Especially since she told the Mountie where to find us."

Minnie giggled nervously and waved her free hand airily about. "Oh, that! I'm sure you misunderstood me when—"

"No." Lesia spoke with barely controlled fury. "I didn't misunderstand you at all." She took a deep breath. *Stay calm.*

"After you were kind enough not to mention our name," Lesia continued, "your daughter told him all about us. Once he registers, my father will be confined to the farm. And he must report to the police once a month. The only misunderstanding is that someone told him we're Austrian citizens." There. She'd said it.

Paul's eyes widened. He looked down at his daughter.

The colour drained from Minnie's face. Her mouth formed a small O before she pressed her lips shut. She did it a second time. Open, shut; open, shut.

She looked just like a fish, Lesia thought. A nasty, disagreeable, smelly fish. She turned to Andrew. "Can we go now?"

Andrew was studying his niece with an expression of pain and disgust. He nodded and raised a hand to Paul. "I'll see you when I get back." He grabbed the reins, flicked them, and then they were off.

Lesia didn't even smile.

Driving through the gate at the Boychuk farm, Lesia could see at least a dozen people ahead of them in line. Some of them had wagons loaded with sacks of seeds.

"We're going to be here forever," she murmured. It was already noon. It would be hours before they headed home.

"There was bound to be a wait." Andrew waved to someone who called a greeting. "Everyone's rushing to get their chores finished. It won't be as long as you think." He took his place in line and secured the oxen. "I'll have you home by dark," he said before wandering off to greet some old friends.

The Boychuk farm reminded Lesia of Paul's homestead. The vegetable garden was huge; the whitewashed house was clean and surrounded by bright yellow and red flowers. Two cows chewed placidly on a small patch of grass. Half a dozen chickens scratched in the dirt nearby, and the branches of two young apple trees sagged with fruit. At the end of the line was the shack where Mr. Boychuk had built his wooden press. It was almost as large as their burdei!

She smiled at a young mother who was struggling to control her children. She greeted an older woman with a nod. The older woman nodded back and nudged her two sacks forward when the line moved. At least she wasn't the only one with a small amount of seeds, Lesia thought gratefully, as she stood in the midst of the crowd and let the talk swell around her. These people were all immigrants, just like her. With her eyes shut, she could almost believe she was back in Shuparka on market day. Back with Baba.

But as the words registered, a cold chill tickled the back of her neck. This wasn't Shuparka at all.

Bishop Budka's letter. So much trouble. Sympathetic to Austria. Enemy aliens. No understanding. Seizing land. Nothing we can do. Rounding them up. Imprisoned.

At the word *imprisoned*, Lesia's stomach turned. The thought of being thrown in jail and losing their land was enough to make her physically ill. In fact, when Andrew came by later with Pearl's basket of food, she couldn't force one bite past her lips.

Canada was the land of milk and honey. The land of opportunities. Surely all this ugliness couldn't be happening. Surely someone had made a mistake.

* * *

Lesia questioned Andrew later, when they were driving home. She'd been right—they had spent the whole day and much of the evening at the Boychuk farm. Dawn wasn't far away now, though the sky was still dark and the moon hung in front of them like a curl of yellow butter.

"What did Bishop Budka say to cause all this trouble?" Everyone had been talking about the bishop who was the head of the Greek Catholic church in Canada.

"When war was first declared, he urged all Austrian subjects to defend the homeland. He told people to go home and report for military duty. Then, when Britain became involved, he urged Ukrainians to fight for Canada and the British Empire. But," Andrew shrugged, "by then, the damage had been done."

The feet of the oxen clomped rhythmically along the dirt path. *Buboom, buboom, buboom.* Just like the pounding of her heart. "What damage?"

He gave her a quick glance before turning his attention back to the road. "The Canadian government is convinced we're on the side of Austria. Since Canada is against Austria, we're the enemy. That's why the Mountie visited you."

"But we've been repressed by the Austrians for years," she said indignantly. "Why would Canada think we're on the same side?"

"Galicia, where you come from, and Bukovyna, where I come from, are Austro-Hungarian Crown lands. Never mind that our nationality is Ukrainian, our citizenship is—or in my case was—Austrian."

Silently, Lesia pondered his words. Then she said, "People are saying that land is being seized. One man even said something about prison."

"War sends people into a panic." Andrew dismissed her concerns with a wave of his hand. "This isn't the homeland. Canadians are basically good people. You've got to remember, many of them have strong ties to Britain. Eastern Europeans are strange to them, Lesia. They need time to get used to us." He gave her a reassuring smile. "But if we do what we're told and stay out of trouble, everything will be fine."

Out of trouble. Out of politics. Where did that leave Ivan? And Paul? Obviously Minnie's father had taken a risk not telling the Mountie about them. "What if the Mountie marches right back and arrests Paul for trying to keep us secret?"

Andrew fumbled with the reins. "Paul can take care of himself. Besides, your Papa is registering. That's all they care about."

"Papa thought you might enlist," she admitted.

One of the oxen was trying to wander off the path, and it took Andrew a minute to coax the animal back into place. "How can I fight the country and people who gave me life for so many years?" he asked. "How can I take a chance that I'd be fighting my cousin? Or old friends?" He shook his head. "I will, if I have to. God knows, I have no dependants to worry about."

The rest of the trip passed in quiet companionship as Andrew and Lesia each pondered their own thoughts. No dependants. She knew Andrew was thinking of his wife. But her thoughts were of war. Of losing land. Of being imprisoned. It was all too much to absorb.

The sky had turned from navy to grey as they neared the Magus homestead. It was warmer than yesterday, she thought as a small bird hovered in front of the wagon before flying into the bushes. No frost today. She glanced at the two tins of oil nestled at her feet. Pray to God it was enough. Pray to God

Papa returned with enough to last them through the winter.

"Nice fence." Andrew complimented as the oxen ploughed through the scrub, the tiny bells around their necks tinkling as they went.

Flushing with pleasure, Lesia stared ahead to the clearing. The light there had an eerie, grey-flushed-with-pink glow. But it wasn't dawn that gave the sky its unusual colour. It was the burning embers of a fire. And sitting beside it, with their backs to the burdei, were two figures.

"Whoa!" Andrew brought the animals to a standstill.

One of the figures turned. "Mama!" Lesia said happily. Her eyes flew to the man who was just starting to turn towards them. "Ivan!" she cried, her heart thumping in a crazy offbeat rhythm of delight. "You're home!"

Chapter Thirteen

"Not Ivan," the man said. "Just me."

"I'm sorry. You looked like my brother from behind." Lesia attempted a smile.

She should have known! Wasyl Goetz and Ivan didn't look at all alike. Still, there was something in the set of his shoulders, the way he turned. How disappointing!

Mama reached for Andrew's hand. "Thank you for bringing her home."

There was a hush in the air. Frowning, Lesia glanced around the clearing. She sniffed. There was no bread baking. The only smell came from the dying embers of the sorry little fire. Instinctively, she knew something was wrong.

"What's happened?" she asked in a whisper.

Mama dropped Andrew's hand and stood just as the sun

crested the horizon, surrounding her in a halo of peach and pink and gold. Her face, already pale, appeared paler. "Oh, Lesia." Her voice broke.

The sun inched into view. Its cheery brightness sliced sharply through the air, mocking the fear that clutched her stomach. "What's happened?" Lesia demanded again.

"It's Ivan." Tears glistened in the corners of Mama's eyes. "He's been taken into custody. In Winnipeg."

The words roared in Lesia's ears. Her knees buckled. Andrew put an arm around her shoulder and settled her on a stump. Her legs felt like potatoes that had been boiled to mush. She shut her eyes and tried to think.

Into custody. Ivan, what have you done?

The sun caressed her face. The dying fire warmed her legs. For a minute she focused on that and shut out all the ugliness. "Why?" she finally whispered.

"He tried to enlist," Wasyl explained. "He was caught lying about his nationality."

Lesia's eyes popped open.

"If he told them he was from Galicia, he knew he'd be classed as an Austrian and disqualified, so he called himself a Russian instead." Mama sank onto a stump beside her and filled in the details. "There were several young men and they were all taken off to jail."

"When?" Lesia asked.

"Two days ago," Wasyl told her. "Three of us escaped, but most are still there."

She didn't care about most. She only cared about Ivan. And Papa! "Papa is in Winnipeg. He can talk to them. He can make them understand."

Mama's shoulders began to shake. She was crying.

"Hush, Mama." Lesia pulled her close and rocked her back and forth. "Everything will be all right. Papa will get Ivan released." With each rock, Lesia's stomach rose and fell, like she was going to be sick.

"Papa . . ." Mama sobbed. "Papa's there too."

Lesia felt light-headed. Dizzy. Confused. "What are you talking about?"

"They brought your Papa in last night, just before I escaped." Wasyl's eyes were dark with pity. "They accused him of supporting the Austrians by sending a large sum of money home."

Lesia gasped. "But that was for Master Stryk. I sent money too." *What if they come after me?*

Beside her, Mama's frail body shook with sobs. Andrew dropped his head into his hands. "Bozhe," he whispered. "Some fine mess this is."

Lesia exploded. "If Ivan had had the common sense not to enlist—to stay out of politics for once in his life—this never would have happened." She turned accusing eyes towards Wasyl Goetz.

Wasyl stuck his chin into the air. "We've been persecuted for years! This was our chance to right wrongs, to fight with Canada. To support our new country. Who wouldn't do it?"

"I'll have to go to Winnipeg and see what I can do," Andrew said.

"He's probably not there any more." Wasyl's anger dissolved into weary resignation. He stood up and began to pace. "The jails are so full of enemy aliens, they're taking men to Brandon."

The internment camp! So what she'd heard at the Boychuk farm *was* true. Dear Lord! Lesia blinked back tears. What were they going to do? Surely Papa and Ivan would be back soon. But if not . . . ? And what if they came for her?

Seizing land. Nothing they can do.

The remembered words turned her hot, then cold, then hot again. If one rumour was true, then perhaps the other one was too. She couldn't risk losing their land. She had to do everything she could to hold on to it.

"We'll need your help." Lesia looked from Andrew to Wasyl. "Both of you."

Wasyl stopped moving and eyed Lesia with suspicion. Andrew nodded and stood.

Mama looked confused. "What do you mean?" she asked.

"We'll have to borrow Andrew's oxen to clear more of our land. It'll go much faster with the animals. Wasyl can help," Lesia added. "No sense in him going back to Winnipeg. They'll be only too happy to throw him into jail."

"Lesia!" Mama looked horrified. "We can't ask Andrew to spare his oxen . . . to spend his time here. What are you thinking?"

"We have six acres left to clear, Mama. If it's not done . . . She hesitated, unable to voice the horror she was imagining. "We just can't give the Canadians any other reason to hound us." *Any other reason to imprison us.*

"But we have until next May," Mama reminded her. "That's lots of time."

Yes, *if Papa and Ivan return*, Lesia thought.

Andrew brushed Mama's comment aside. "No time like

now," he said. "I could be back with the walking plough tomorrow afternoon. We might not get all six acres cleared, but we'll do the best we can. With hard work and a little luck, we'll make a good dent in them."

Mama was clearly embarrassed. "There's no need for that. This is all a mistake. Canada is a democracy. I'm sure the men will be home in days."

"It *is* a mistake," Andrew said gently. "And Canada is a democracy. But it's wartime. Everything changes then."

Mama nodded. "I know. And I appreciate the offer, but Gregory would be furious to come home and see that you had done his work for him. The man has pride." She smiled rue-fully. "Sometimes too much. But right now, our pride is all we have left."

Lesia and Andrew exchanged looks. "I understand you had a Mountie here?" Andrew asked.

"Yes."

"Did he say anything about cultivating your land?"

"Yes," Mama said a second time.

"Government orders?"

Mama nodded.

"They're going to be watching, Ahafia." Andrew bent down until he was eye to eye with Mama. "We may not like it, we may not understand it, but if you don't show improve-ments, like building a house or cultivating the land, they'll take your section back. It's the law. And now, with the war on, they're going to be even stricter."

"We don't have the money to build a house," Mama cried. "Not yet."

"But we can clear the land, and that's a sure sign of improvement." He hesitated. "You can't risk losing everything for the sake of Gregory's pride."

"Very well," Mama said softly. "We'll accept your help."

Chapter Fourteen

October 29, 1914

The Magus homestead

"Wake up, Lessie!" Sonia's breath was hot on her ear.

"Mmm-hmmmm." Lesia wrapped her arm around the small child and snuggled against her back. "Soon." Mornings were so cold now even the thought of getting up made her shiver. Besides, when she slept she could forget the horror of life, the fear that she had somehow failed everyone by coming to Canada. "One more minute."

Sonia pulled out of her arms and sat up. "The white powder is on the ground. Look."

Lesia tossed the thin blanket aside, grabbed her coat and wrapped it around her shoulders.

Sonia ran to the window and peered through the wavy glass. "See!"

"Shhh." Lesia held a cautionary finger to her lips and

directed a worried glance towards Mama and Adam. Relieved to see that they were still sleeping, she joined Sonia.

After drifting from the sky for days but never settling, snow now clung like a thick coating of flour to the ground, the trees, the woodpile. Andrew had told her she would wake to winter one morning, and he had been right. Trouble was, she'd thought she had more time to prepare.

"We have to hurry and get the cabbages in." She sat Sonia down with a small piece of bread.

"I good at helping," the little girl whispered back.

Keeping one eye on Mama and Adam, who slept on top of the oven, Lesia grabbed the small pieces of wood she'd brought in last night and laid them on the still-glowing embers. They caught almost immediately. Praise to Mother Mary herself for Andrew and Wasyl's oven!

So much had happened in the last month. Andrew had gone back to his farm, where he'd gathered equipment and rounded up four more men. Together, they had pulled and sweated and grunted their way across the prairie, clearing the last six acres so fast Lesia was dizzy with the speed of it.

Soon after, Wasyl and the four other men had disappeared. That's when Andrew had told her he was knocking out the side of the burdei for a built-in clay oven. Panicked at the thought of losing any part of the burdei, she'd argued against it. But Andrew had patiently drawn a picture on one of her precious pieces of paper. He had shown her how there would be an opening for baking, a metal plate for cooking and a long, flat top that would give someone a warm place to sleep at night. It wouldn't be as fancy as a store-bought tin stove, he warned, but it would do.

Lesia couldn't imagine when they would ever have money for a store-bought tin stove, so she said yes to Andrew's idea.

Sure that the fire had caught, Lesia gulped down a piece of bread and hustled Sonia outside, giving thanks once again for Papa's window and the crude wooden door Wasyl had nailed together. She shuddered to think how cold they would be without them.

The world was beautiful and clean and pure. It was a hush of white, a crunch of footfall, a taste of crispness. If only Papa and Ivan could be there to see it. *If only, if only.*

"Look! Look at me." Sonia jumped up and down, making little footprints everywhere she went.

Lesia stuck her tongue into the air. Small white flakes melted with tiny stings as they hit her mouth and her cheeks.

Everyone said winter on the prairies was harsh and unforgiving, but this wasn't so bad. She could still see grass under the snow. And the woodpile was barely brushed with white.

"Only one itty bitty egg, Lessie."

"It's probably the last one till spring." She tossed the birds a handful of poppy seeds and headed towards the creek.

Snow had turned the shrubs into strange and magical shapes; tree branches looked like twisted black-and-white pencils against the sky. "Let's check the traps."

All three were empty. It had been weeks since they'd caught a rabbit. And Papa had used the last of the shotgun shells before he'd left for Winnipeg.

It took Lesia a long time to carry all the cabbages inside. By then, Mama had fed Adam and was starting to shred the large heads. "Traps empty?" She raised an eyebrow.

Mutely, Lesia nodded.

Mama's hands moved rhythmically over the cabbage. "Perhaps today Papa and Ivan will return." Her eyes glistened with hope. "Or maybe Andrew will come with our flour."

There had been no word about Papa and Ivan since the day they had learned of their imprisonment. Andrew had said he would ask again when he went to town with their eggs.

Their tears had stopped long ago. Mama relied on a quiet faith to see her through the days; Lesia wrestled with a bitter combination of anger, fear and constant worry.

Where were they? How were they? What was going to happen to them?

Forcing her thoughts away, Lesia began layering salt and cabbage in the crock. Andrew had brought both the last time he had visited. Egg money, he'd said. But he'd also returned with a top for the oven and sweets for Sonia. He was doing too much . . . spending too much from his own pocket.

When he had left last time with three dozen eggs, Lesia had dared not ask him to buy shotgun shells. Instead, she'd made a point of saying, "Flour only, no extras."

But if he did bring extras, Lord God, she prayed it would be the shells.

⁂

By the time Andrew showed up more than a week later, the woodpile, the garden and every tuft of grass were buried under mounds of white. The snow muffled sounds, so Lesia didn't hear a thing until his loud voice boomed through the burdei door one morning.

"You awake in there?"

Lesia grinned and dropped the square of burlap she was turning into a shirt. "Of course we're awake." Mama covered up a nursing Adam and Lesia pulled the makeshift door open. "Come in."

The cold air clung to his coat like a blanket. "Where do you want this?" He was balancing a sack of flour on one shoulder.

"Here." Lesia helped him put it in the corner.

"There's more." He disappeared outside again.

Sonia clapped her hands in anticipation. Mama smiled. Lesia's breath caught. Shotgun shells?

There were no shells. Instead, Pearl and Paul had sent jars of soup, loaves of bread and a very small offering of rich, pale cream. "There'll be no more till spring now," Andrew said apologetically as he handed it over to Mama.

Next he reached into the folds of his sheepskin coat. "Something for you, miss." He presented Sonia with a multicoloured rag doll. "And for you." He handed Mama two skeins of wool, one a rich red and the other a brilliant blue. He turned to Lesia.

"I said no extras." She was embarrassed by his charity; now she understood how Papa felt at times like this.

"This is not an extra." He pulled two small metal hinges from his pocket. "To let the door open and close with ease."

Then he pulled a piece of paper from the other pocket of his heavy sheepskin coat and handed it to her.

Lesia stared at her name written in large, bold script on the front of an official-looking beige envelope. *Lesia Magus, Hazelridge, Manitoba.* Fingers shaking, she released the flap and pulled out a single sheet of paper.

Dearest Lesia, she read silently. *Papa and I are together in the*

Brandon camp. We have not been beaten, nor have we starved to death. But I will tell you the truth and you decide whether to tell Mama.

There are hundreds of us and not enough beds to go around. We get fed three times a day, and I know I should be grateful. But it is slop, not fit to feed to animals. Pails of meat and bread stew. More bread-and-water broth than anything, and what meat there is comes slimed with green. We've had potatoes four times—each time they looked like soot and smelled much worse. And twice we've had turnip—the pieces were so hard you could cut down trees with them.

Every day we are outside. First for exercise marches, until we almost drop from exhaustion, and then we are forced to work. Guards stand with their bayonets almost touching us. If we slow down they prod us like oxen. After a while the cold is enough to make grown men weep. Still, we carry on. We work ten hours and are paid twenty-five cents a day. At night we talk of our families to keep up our spirits. We plan for the future and pray there will be one.

They tell us we may send and receive eight letters a month. I am grateful for the chance to write. And I am more grateful than you will ever know for that paper and pencil Andrew gave you. I hope there is enough left that you may answer me. Papa is so proud you can read and write and he begs you to take care of Mama and the children. Give them all a hug for us, especially my new brother Adam, whom I hope to meet very soon.

Your loving brother, Ivan.

Bozhe! Her eyes filled with tears. *Prodded like oxen. Meat slimed with green.* She pretended to read the letter a second time, though her eyes were too blurred to focus.

"It's from Ivan," she said softly when she could finally speak around the lump in her throat. "And from Papa."

"What do they say?" Mama demanded.

Lesia recapped the letter, exaggerating what good there was and minimizing the bad.

When she was finished, Mama looked relieved. "How wonderful that they're warm and safe and well fed. I'm sure God, in His infinite wisdom, will send them home to us soon."

Lesia and Andrew exchanged looks. "Perhaps," she said softly, not believing it for a minute. "Perhaps."

* * *

The letters between the homestead and the camp came steadily all through November and into December. Lesia tucked them into Baba's special box, often taking them out and rereading them late at night, before bed. The weather prevented Andrew from visiting very often, but when he did, he always brought a letter. And Lesia always had a letter ready to send back.

Those first letters were the best. Everyone was deliriously happy to be in touch and hopeful that they would soon be together again. But as time went on, the letters became predictable and monotonous, just like the depressing greyness of the sky after months of brilliant sun. After a while, entire paragraphs were censored, and, try as she might, Lesia could never make out the words.

We pray for an end to this situation, Ivan wrote. *Papa says borrowing money is wrong, no matter what. I have tried to talk to him, but he refuses to reason.* Harsh black strokes prevented her from reading four lines before the letter resumed. *There is talk that soon they will allow visitors. We pray this will happen. Your brother, Ivan.*

We think of you always, and Mama and the children send love, Lesia would respond. *It has been weeks since we've had fresh meat. It is too cold to go outside to check the traps and we have no money for shotgun shells. The flour Andrew brought is dwindling, and our sauerkraut is almost gone. I paid Andrew for the doctor's bill with the last of the egg money. We dream of fresh eggs and sunshine. We dream of you home safe where you belong. Love, Lesia.*

Once Ivan realized his letters were being censored, he got crafty and the black lines disappeared. *I am glad you have enough fresh meat,* he wrote. *And that your sauerkraut is plentiful. We are all well. The guards are as nice as Michal Stryk. We are building a fence. It is easy work and the pay is good. The food is plentiful and I am sure we will soon be home. Visits are allowed once a month and I really hope* (this he had underlined twice) *you will come. Thinking of you, Ivan.*

Lesia read between the lines. Life in the camp was harsh and unfriendly. The guards were mean, the work horrific. She didn't need to go there and witness for herself the shame and humiliation. No. Besides, she was needed at home. She was the only one who could set the traps, and she didn't dare send Mama out into the cold to check them. Her health was still too fragile.

We are cold, she wrote back, *so we have cut down your sheepskin coat to fit Sonia. She's growing and had nothing left to wear outside. I've made some thick boots from the flour sack but they offer little protection from the cold. Last week I caught a rabbit. Our first in three weeks. Please tell Papa things are desperate. Our food is just about gone. Mama's milk has dried up and Adam is as thin as a rail. He has almost no energy left to cry. The cold slices us like a knife cutting butter. It leaves us perpetually shaking. Even the chickens are too cold to be outside. That towering woodpile you were so proud of is near the ground now. The Korols give us food when they can, and Andrew too, but I do not like to take advantage. I would rather borrow money than accept so many gifts. Surely Papa will understand. Please answer soon, Lesia.*

Soon enough, Lesia had her answer.

No debt, Ivan wrote. *Winter is long in this place but they are still allowing visitors one Friday a month. Men are being moved almost daily. Some to Kapuskasing, some to a place called Banff. Please come and see us while you still can. Ivan.*

"If you go, perhaps they will let Ivan and Papa come home with you," Mama whispered later that night as they sat wrapped in blankets in front of the oven.

"I don't think so," Lesia whispered back. Adam slept, but Sonia peered over her blanket as the two women talked. In spite of her worry, Lesia had to smile at those large blue eyes taking it all in. "Go to sleep, little one," she told the child.

She turned back to Mama. "I'm going to borrow money from Andrew," she said. "To buy shells for the shotgun."

"Papa forbids it."

"Papa isn't here. He doesn't have to know."

"Lesia!"

Why had she told Mama the truth when she'd read the last letter? Why hadn't she lied and pretended Papa had given his permission? She knew it was for the same reason she'd finally told her things were not wonderful at the internment camps: she had to share her pain. "We have to, Mama. It's our only hope."

"No. I forbid it on Papa's behalf."

"Mama, you're not being reasonable! We need fresh meat. What other choice do we have?"

"Go to the camp and see the men," Mama insisted. "We'll be staying at the Korols' over Christmas, you can go then. You'll convince the authorities to let them out, Lesia, I know you will."

"They aren't going to listen to me. I'm a nobody. Besides, Brandon's hundreds of miles away, Mama. It's impossible to walk there in this cold."

"You'll have to take the train. Andrew offered to pay your fare. I accepted."

"You won't let me borrow money for shells but you'll take money for train fare?" The words burst out of her. Sonia giggled and popped her head over the blanket. After settling her sister a second time, Lesia turned disbelieving eyes to Mama. "A small package of shells is less than a dollar. The train to Brandon has to cost ten or twelve dollars."

"It's eight dollars return."

All this charity was getting to be too much. "Oh, Mama, how could you?"

"How could I not?" Mama met her gaze unflinchingly. "Andrew offered it as a gift and I accepted. It's easy to lock a man away, but not so easy to turn your back on his daughter when she stands there begging for his release."

Mama expected her to beg?

"Andrew will drop you at the train in Hazelridge. You'll make the connection in Winnipeg and be in Brandon just after noon on Friday, the sixth," Mama said. "That leaves you several hours to get to the camp and still make the train back in time for the celebration."

Lesia gasped."You'd have me go there on the Holy Eve?"

"If that's what it takes."

"You go, Mama." The thought of seeing beloved Papa and Ivan behind bars was enough to make her sick with shame and full of loathing. Loathing for herself. Why had she thought coming to Canada would make life better?

"I can't leave Adam and Sonia for that long," Mama explained. "And Andrew offered money for only one fare. You must go, Lesia. If they are moved to another camp, we might never see them again."

Bozhe! Couldn't Mama understand? "What if . . ." Her lower lip quivered. "What if they keep me there?" she whispered thickly.

"They can't do that. You've done nothing wrong."

"Neither have Papa and Ivan."

Mama stared at Lesia a long time before dropping her eyes. "I don't understand this mess."

"Neither do I." But there was one thing Lesia did understand. She *had* to go to Brandon. She had to go and talk some sense into Papa. She also had to go because, Lord God forbid, if they were moved and she never saw them again, she'd have more pain, more guilt and more reasons to loathe herself.

Chapter Fifteen

January 6, 1915

Brandon, Manitoba

The cold air stung Lesia's eyes and made her chest ache with each breath. The bitter wind swirled the snow into whirling dervishes at her feet. Clutching the basket of goodies Pearl had assembled that morning, she stared at the grey wooden building.

The Brandon Winter Fair Arena. Papa's and Ivan's jail.

It was low to the ground, only a storey and a half, but it was huge, five or six times the size of Master Stryk's mansion. Unlike the landowner's mansion, however, two armed guards stood watch on either side of large double doors.

Lesia had been worried about getting lost when she got off the train. Andrew had told her to simply ask for directions, but in the end she hadn't needed to. There had been a number of other Ukrainians on the train from Winnipeg to Brandon, and, by the bits of conversation she had overheard, Lesia knew they were heading for the same place.

Many of these people carried baskets or packages wrapped with string. Their clothes were worn, their shoulders were hunched, their faces were filled with fear. Just like her. And just like her, they were taking advantage of the last visiting day before Holy Eve.

Lesia reached the bottom of the stairs and joined the line of people waiting to be cleared by the guards.

"Hurry up, hurry up!" a voice from behind grumbled in Ukrainian.

She resisted the urge to turn around and flee. Instead, she inched her way towards the top of the stairs, wishing she could see what the guards were doing. Her view was blocked by the broad shoulders of a woman who was struggling to control two active, red-haired sons.

Finally, it was Lesia's turn.

A barrel-chested man with a huge curled moustache put out his hand. Shifting the basket, she fumbled for her citizenship papers. He rolled his eyes and made a snickering comment to the other guard. Both men laughed. She studied the shiny gold buttons on his blue coat, the starched collar that hugged his neck. How embarrassing to be treated this way.

He spoke gruffly. In English. She looked at his mouth and tried to understand what he was saying. She couldn't.

He spoke again, and she wanted to sink into the ground.

"Open the parcel and show him." It was the same Ukrainian voice that had grumbled at her to hurry up. "They check everything."

She pulled the cloth back and held up the basket for inspection. The guard pawed through the pyrohy, the cookies and the crock of honey before resting his hand on the bread. With a nasty wink at Lesia, he picked it up, turned it upside down and shoved his fist through the crust to the soft dough inside. Withdrawing his hand, he dropped the bread into the basket, shook the crumbs away and spoke to the man beside him. They both laughed again.

How could he do such a horrible thing? Trembling, Lesia covered the basket and fought back tears.

"Tell him who you are visiting," the voice from behind hissed.

"Gregory and Ivan Magus," she said, hugging the basket tight.

The other guard studied a large brown clipboard. Lesia held her breath. When he took his thick black pen and scratched off two names, she let it out. He returned her papers and motioned her forward.

She was inside. And the sudden warmth after the wind and cold made her nose tingle. She loosened the knot in her scarf, pulled it away from her face and joined the line that snaked its way down the hall. It was lovely and warm. Strange that a place so full of evil could feel so wonderful. And be so bright.

The woman with the two young boys smiled over her shoulder. Hesitantly, Lesia smiled back. "What do we do now?" she murmured.

"When you get in, say what you have to say quickly," she answered softly. The two boys giggled and jostled each other and the taller of the two fell laughing to the floor. "They only give us a few minutes, and they are angry with us for bringing gifts when their Christmas is already over." With a grimace of disapproval, the woman grabbed the boy by his collar and yanked him off the floor.

Lesia was shocked until she saw a guard in a stiff green uniform glaring at the young child. He spoke harshly and gestured with his bayonet. The woman nodded, dropped her eyes, pulled her young son close and began to scold him.

He was only a child. But he was a *Ukrainian* child. Lesia's face filled with heat. To be so hated, and all because they were Ukrainian. At first she was mortified, ashamed. They were not good enough for Canada, for this land of milk and honey. They were not worthy of the great gifts the prairie soil could provide. But then anger replaced shame. *They* were ploughing and cultivating virgin land. *Their men* were building the rail line. Enemies of the Canadian people? Hardly that.

Yet the guards seemed to think so. Some patrolled the hall; others stood under tremendously large electric lights and stared fiercely at the line. If people moved even slightly or spoke too loudly, they were prodded with long, black bayonets.

How dare they treat people this way? She challenged the blue-eyed guard with a defiant stare. His eyes flickered ominously, but then he looked away. Lesia began to breathe again.

Turning a corner, she caught sight of rows and rows of narrow cots, each one covered with a blanket. Not only did they have heat and light, she thought with a tug of envy, they had beds and blankets too!

How could she think such things? No doubt Papa and Ivan would give anything to go home and sleep on the cold floor with the rest of them.

Lesia followed the crowd through a maze of hallways, up one flight of stairs and down another. And then, before she had time to worry about finding her way out again, she was being pushed forward by the others into a large, open room.

Into a crowd of babbling people.

And Papa's arms.

"I've missed you, moye sonechko." He grabbed her close before she had time to get a good look at him.

Her arms flew around his neck; she clung tightly. "Oh, Papa, I've missed you too!" Loosening her grip, she stepped back. Her smile slipped. The noise in the room receded. *Papa?*

His eyes were bleak, defeated. His shoulders slumped, his hands trembled. His salt-and-pepper hair had turned completely white. He was a mere shell of the man she'd hugged at the end of September.

"Lesia!" Ivan called. She turned, prepared for the worst. But aside from the cynical smile, which was a little more sullen than usual, her brother looked the same as always.

"I'm glad you came." He squeezed her hand. "Thank you." Lesia swallowed her tears. Ivan never thanked her for anything.

People were breaking into smaller groups, spreading out through the large room. Voices were dropping. Confidences were being exchanged.

Ivan led them to a far wall. Guards eyed them carefully but did not stop them.

"How is everyone?" Papa demanded.

Hungry. Scared. Worried. "We're all fine," Lesia lied. She couldn't add to the pain in his eyes. "Mama sends her love." That much was true. "And how are you? Are they treating you well?"

Papa was silent. Ivan spoke for him. "I suppose." He gestured to one of the passing guards. "We're warm, we're dry, we're fed. We have a bed and a blanket. Our biggest problem is boredom." His eyebrows linked in a fierce frown. "Too much time to think about the injustice of it all."

An awkward silence fell. Lesia shifted nervously from one foot to the other. *Just a few minutes.* "Papa, I must borrow money. You see, we—"

Ivan cut her off. "That's good, Lesia, good!" His voice was loud and false. His eyes were fastened on something over her shoulder.

Her neck prickled. She whirled around. The blue-eyed guard smirked cruelly down at her. He was close enough to touch. Contemptuously, his gaze travelled from the top of her head to the bottom of her burlap-covered feet. Then he sauntered away.

She turned back. "I *must* borrow money, Papa. We need shells for the shotgun. We have some flour but the sack is getting low. Pearl and Paul give us bread and sometimes potatoes. Andrew was selling our eggs but the chickens have stopped laying for the winter. He was the one who paid for the trip today. He insisted on it being a gift. You've always said that relying on charity is worse than borrowing money and paying it back."

"No more debt, Lesia!" A flash of Papa's old spirit returned. "We're through with it. Andrew has been paid. So has Master Stryk."

Lesia bit her tongue. *And what good did that do?* she wanted to ask. *If you hadn't mailed that money, they wouldn't have arrested you and charged you with supporting the enemy. You wouldn't be here right now!*

But she couldn't blame Papa. She had mailed money to Master Stryk too. Only she hadn't got caught doing it. Not yet, at least. "Papa, you must understand, we—"

"So Mama is well," Ivan's voice boomed out again. "I'm glad to hear it."

There was another guard near. "Yes!" Lesia spoke with forced cheerfulness. "And Adam too," she noted.

"Adam!" Grief settled in the creases of Papa's face like a dusting of snow settling on land. "Will I ever see my Adam again?" His eyes filled with tears.

"Shhh." Ivan frowned. "Do you want to call attention?"

But the guard was gone.

Just a few more minutes. "Papa," Lesia said gently, "we are not fine. Sonia cries all the time from hunger. There's no milk for Adam, he's losing weight. And Mama is coughing again. Borrowing money is the only answer, Papa."

Wordlessly he shook his head. He looked away.

"Ivan." Lesia appealed to her brother. "Talk to him."

But her brother shook his head too. "No debt, Lesia. It's too risky."

Not Ivan too? Lesia's anger spilled out like flax seeds falling from a sack. "What do you know of risk?" Her voice trembled with frustration. "You have food and warmth and a dry place to sleep at night. We are freezing in the burdei, and starving."

"Borrowing money means you must trust someone," Ivan said. "We can trust no one. Not even other Ukrainians."

"We can trust Andrew."

"Yes, but if someone finds out he helped, he could be in trouble. Or we could lose our land."

"That won't happen."

"There are no guarantees, Lesia." Ivan's smile was humourless. "Surely you know that by now."

She was silent. A picture of nasty Minnie Korol slid into her mind.

"Without land," Ivan said, "we are nothing."

"Without food, we will starve!"

Ivan leaned close so Papa was out of earshot. "Borrow some shells from Andrew or Paul," he whispered. "Make them promise to tell no one. At least then you can use the shotgun."

It wasn't all she wanted, but it was a start. "As long as I can stay outside long enough to hunt," she said. "It's so cold, my fingers and toes are almost always numb."

"It won't take you long to catch something," Ivan predicted. "They say the rabbits practically come up and beg to be shot in the cold weather. Sometimes prairie chickens too." He turned to Papa. "As soon as this guard passes, I want you to bend down, pretend you're scratching your ankle and undo your boots."

Papa nodded.

What was Ivan thinking? Lesia wondered.

"Then you'll stand beside Papa," he said to her, staring down at the chunks of burlap she had wrapped around and around what was left of her old boots. "It doesn't look like you'll have any trouble slipping those off without bending over," he said.

"Probably not," Lesia admitted. "But why?"

Ivan didn't answer. The blue-eyed guard with the nasty smirk sauntered by. When they could see his back, Ivan spoke. "Now, Papa!" Papa bent over and went to work.

"You're going to need Papa's boots to get out in the snow,"

Ivan explained. "They'll be big, but you can stuff them with rags. When you're not using them, Mama can."

"What will Papa use?" Her father straightened. His boots were positioned inconspicuously behind him.

"Yours."

Lesia's eyes widened. "There's nothing to them. Besides, they'll be too small."

"They'll do for now," her brother said. "When they see his boots are falling apart, maybe they'll find him another pair." His lips twisted into a mirthless grin. "Or let him stay inside when the weather's at its worst."

Watching carefully for guards, Lesia slowly worked the old burlap-wrapped boots off her feet. It was a long process, but eventually she was able to nudge them towards Papa. He, in turn, slid his boots to her. Once they were hidden under her skirt, she took her time sliding her feet into them. Finally, with Ivan shielding her, she bent over and did them up.

As she straightened, a bell started to ring. Several children began to cry. "Two more minutes," yelled a barrel-chested guard with a brown moustache. "Two minutes!"

Ivan translated. *So soon?*

Papa reached out and grabbed her hands. "Moye sonechko, please know that I love you! I love all of you more than life itself." His eyes filled and one lone tear trickled down his cheek. "Tell Mama I'm sorry for what has happened. Tell her I'll make it up to her when I get home. Tell her I love her. And . . ." His voice cracked. "And tell her I pray for her." He turned to the wall.

Ivan reached for her hand. "Lesia, you know I've done some foolish things in my life. I've taken many risks. I know you're very brave and you feel great responsibility. I'm proud of what you've accomplished on the land. But whatever you do, do *not* borrow money from anyone." His eyes tunnelled into her. "The safety of our land could depend on it." He squeezed her hand. "Promise me?"

"It's time," bellowed the same barrel-chested guard. "Please leave by the east doors. Leave by the east doors."

"You must leave now." Ivan said. "But first promise me!"

Lesia's heart sank to the bottom of her new boots. "I promise," she said thickly.

She forced herself to leave without looking back. What was worse? she wondered as she followed a crying woman out the door. Making that horrible promise or wondering when—*if*—she would ever see Papa and Ivan again?

Chapter Sixteen

Pearl's house was warm with bodies and the rich smells of the Holy Eve feast. Tiny fingertips scratched away the frost as the children peered out the large front window and into the dark sky for a first glimpse of the beloved Star of Bethlehem. Not only would it signal the end of fasting and the start of feasting, but whoever saw it first would have good fortune for an entire year.

Lesia smiled as Sonia, her tiny shoulders quivering with excitement, gently pushed her way forward to take her place beside Victoria, Pearl's middle daughter. *If only I were that young again. If only I could believe in good fortune.*

But she couldn't.

She cradled Adam in her arms and wished her brother hadn't

picked this time to fall peacefully asleep. A fussy baby would have left her no time to think about today's visit.

About Papa. Ivan. And her promise not to borrow money.

Bozhe, Bozhe! If only Papa had listened to reason. If only Ivan hadn't lost his fight and become so wary. If only Canada had welcomed them with open arms, instead of locking their men away like common criminals.

We are all equal in the eyes of God. Baba's words echoed in her mind. Could Baba have been wrong?

"It is magical, is it not?" Mama stacked the braided kolachi on the table and centred a candle in the middle of the top loaf.

"It is," Lesia agreed.

The table was laid with a layer of loose hay and a sparkling clean white cloth topped by a colourful embroidered one. There was more hay scattered on the floor. Farm tools were placed in the corners of the room to symbolize the importance of the land. Candles were everywhere, just waiting to be lit. And the air was thick with the savoury smells of the twelve meatless dishes Ukrainians everywhere consumed on the Holy Eve. Treasured dishes like kutia and pyrohy, borsch and holubtsi, stewed mushrooms and prune torte.

The room, the food, even the smells were all more elaborate and more beautiful than any Holy Eve the Magus family had celebrated in Shuparka. It made Lesia mad. And she felt guilty about her feelings.

Mama sighed. "If only Papa and Ivan were here."

"They send their love," Lesia said again.

Mama's cheeks were pale in the candlelight; her eyes were sad and defeated. She had been so sure Lesia would bring them back. "Have you told me everything, Lesia?"

"Everything," she lied.

Intently, Mama studied Lesia's face. Satisfied with what she saw, she nodded and turned away.

She could tell Mama all about the camp itself, but she couldn't bring herself to tell her how terrible Papa looked. Instead, she'd said he was in fine health and full of good cheer.

Surely God would forgive her?

"The animals have been fed," Paul boomed as he led Andrew and Wasyl through the front door. Cold flakes of white snow swirled about their feet.

"Good! Good!" Pearl tucked a sleeping Mary into the cradle. Ancient legend decreed that on this holiest of nights animals were given the gift of human speech and could complain or rejoice to God for the way in which their human owners treated them. They were always fed some of the delicacies first, as a reminder of their importance to the family.

"The didukh!" Anastasia exclaimed when she caught sight of her Uncle Andrew. The children watched as Andrew ceremoniously hung the large sheaf of wheat symbolizing the gathering of friends and family.

"To the family," the men said.

"To the family," the women and children repeated.

And then everyone hurried back to their appointed chores. The children to watch out the window. The women to dish up the food. And the men to wash for the upcoming feast.

"Are you sure you're all right?" Andrew stood so close his arm touched Adam's blanket. Lesia glanced nervously towards Minnie, who glared at them as though they were talking about her.

"I'm fine," she whispered back. Andrew had known something was wrong the moment he had picked her up at the train station in Hazelridge. Wordlessly, he'd studied her white face. Wordlessly, he'd noticed the boots. But he'd said nothing about it until they were nearing Paul's homestead. Then he'd come right out and asked her about Papa.

Not Ivan. Papa. As though he'd known. Perhaps the boots had given it away.

That's when the lump had grown in Lesia's throat. And it hadn't moved since. She hadn't lied to Andrew, but she hadn't told him the truth, either. How could she describe the pain she'd felt in seeing Papa so beaten down, the humiliation that scorched her soul when the guards treated them like dirt?

"I'm here if you want to talk," he said.

"Maybe later." The lump in her throat was so big it was hard to talk around it.

"The star!" Luka yelled. "I see it!"

"Me too!" exclaimed Sonia.

"And me!" said Symon.

Everyone began talking at once. Voices were raised in excitement.

Could Papa and Ivan see the star? Lesia wondered. Did they have a window from which to observe the night sky? And did the guards understand their men still deserved to celebrate the holiest of nights?

Through a blur of tears, Lesia could see Paul holding up his hand. "Christ is born!" he said reverently.

"Khrystos rodyvsia!" everyone repeated.

A lone tear snaked its way down her cheek.

"Let us glorify him," Paul said.

"Slavim Yoho!" everyone echoed.

"Come," Paul urged, "be seated while I light the candles."

Swiftly, before anyone could see, Andrew reached out and wiped the tear away. "Be brave," he said quietly.

Lesia wasn't sure what made her more uncomfortable, Andrew's touch or the fact that he seemed to know what she was thinking. She put Adam in the makeshift cradle beside Mary, took her place beside Wasyl and waited for Paul to recite the prayer.

"Dearest Lord in Heaven, we thank you for our many blessings. We are grateful for our harvest, for the health of our family and for the food we are about to eat. We are grateful, too, for the new friends you have led to us, Wasyl Goetz and the Magus family, all of whom are here with us tonight."

Not *all*, Lesia thought.

"Dearest God Almighty," Paul continued, "we say a special prayer for Gregory and Ivan Magus. We know they are with us in spirit and we pray that they are returned to us quickly and safely."

Lesia wouldn't look at the empty seat that loomed at one end of the table. It served as a reminder that even though the men were not there in body, they were there in spirit. It was also there for Baba, to encourage her spirit to come down from Heaven and join them in celebration.

"Finally, Lord, in this year of political turmoil, we pray for peace. For our family, for Canada and most especially for our homeland, Ukraine. We ask that your love and spirit guide all of those in positions of authority as we await an end to this conflict. Amen."

"Amen," everyone repeated.

Pearl stood. Ceremoniously, she waved a long stick of grey

incense over the food in blessing. Its exotic scent wafted across the table. Reverently, she put it aside and sat down.

Then Paul stood. The children were wide-eyed. They giggled in anticipation. He reached for a handful of kutia, the luscious sweet of boiled wheat, poppy seeds and honey. His eyes twinkled. He raised his hand and threw it at the ceiling. It stuck! Everyone began to laugh and clap. The gesture ensured good luck and a healthy harvest for the coming year. With that taken care of, the babbling began.

"It smells wonderful!"

"I want extra nuts."

"I don't want kutia, I want jellied fish instead."

"In time. In time."

"I'm starving," Minnie said.

Lesia watched and listened as the kutia was ceremoniously passed around. *Starving?* She shot a sideways glance in Minnie's direction. *She* hadn't known a day of starvation in her life.

Not like the rest of them.

Beside her, Wasyl tapped his glass with a spoon. "To our hosts!" he said. "Thank you for including us in your Christmas festivities."

Lesia raised her glass along with the rest of them, but she wouldn't meet Wasyl's eyes. Looking at him was a reminder that he'd got away. And Ivan hadn't.

"Do you like them?" Wasyl whispered in Lesia's ear, gesturing to the tall goblets. The cut-crystal stems gleamed in the candlelight.

She held one in the palm of her hand and pretended great interest in the way it was shaped. "It's very nice." Slowly she put it back down. In fact, it was beyond nice. It was the kind of thing that had been locked away at Master Stryk's estate.

"I bought them." Wasyl's voice was loud, boastful.

"Pardon?" She turned to him in surprise. Gifts were often exchanged at Christmas, but nothing so elaborate. She thought of the belts she had woven for Andrew and Pearl. They looked like nothing beside the crystal.

He grinned and stuck out his chest. "I bought them for Paul."

"And for the rest of us, I hope," Minnie pouted. Lesia had noticed with amusement that she'd rushed to grab the seat on the other side of Wasyl. As far as she was concerned, the two of them could have each other.

"Of course," he said gallantly. "Nothing is too good for your family, especially your father. He's been a tremendous help to me."

"I've seen you three having great long conversations in the barn. Don't you get cold?" Minnie teased.

"Cold is the least of our problems." Wasyl passed the kutia to Lesia. "Thank the Lord for your father. He's made some very helpful suggestions about getting along in Canada."

Lesia glanced at Paul, who was dishing up the borsch. A tiny shiver wormed its way down her back. Bozhe, she hoped Wasyl wouldn't lead Paul astray too! But he wouldn't. Paul was too smart for that.

The nuttiness of the steaming kutia filled her nostrils. Her mouth began to water; she was so hungry she must be careful not to overeat. Papa's face floated before her eyes. And Ivan's. Guilt tightened her throat. *How can I eat and enjoy this when they are locked away?*

Well, Ivan and Papa had a bed and a blanket and food to eat

every night. Which was a lot more than she and Mama and the young ones had.

Her teeth sank into the sweet softness of the boiled wheat, the slight crunch of the poppy seeds and nuts. Ah, kutia! Baba's favourite dish of all time.

"Where did you get them?" Minnie asked. "The glasses, I mean." Without looking down the table, Lesia just knew the girl was batting her eyes in Wasyl's direction. She could hear it in her voice.

"At the pawnshop in Winnipeg," Wasyl said importantly. "There are lots of good buys. With the war and all, people need money."

They needed money. Wary but curious, Lesia asked, "What's a pawnshop?"

"When you need money, you take your valuables there. Things that are worth a lot of money."

Papa hadn't said a thing about pawnshops. Too bad she had no valuables to pawn.

"They give you cash in exchange." A few poppy seeds flew from his mouth as he spoke. "Everyone does it."

Lesia leaned away. Not only were his manners crude, he wasn't trustworthy. Just look at the trouble Ivan had gotten into hanging around him. How could she believe what he said?

Minnie giggled. "Maybe you could take me one day."

"What did you pawn?" Lesia asked him.

"Nothing. You can buy things too. After a while, if people don't buy their valuables back, they're sold off for a song. There are mouth organs and fur coats and jewels. Dishes and silver and crystal. I even saw a piano."

Across the table, Mama finished helping Sonia and looked up. "A piano? Really?"

Wasyl nodded. "Really."

There was silence as the borsch was passed down, followed by pyrohy and fish and holubtsi.

If only she had something valuable to take to the pawnshop. But Lesia had nothing at all. She was going to have to learn to hunt, and pray she could catch enough to feed the family through the winter.

When the dishes were finally cleared and the carols were sung, Lesia shyly handed Andrew and Pearl the colourful belts she'd woven from the wool she'd found in Baba's trunk.

Andrew proclaimed it the nicest gift he'd ever received. Pearl said she hadn't seen anything as nice since leaving the homeland.

"When the other women see these," Pearl continued, her fingers tracing the design, "they are going to want them too."

Lesia's heart jumped. Perhaps she could take belts to the pawnshop! They were valuable enough. But as valuable as silver or furs? No.

"Could you make me three more?" the older woman asked. "For Minnie, Anastasia and Victoria?"

Minnie peered over her mother's shoulder. Her mouth curled in disgust.

"I'll pay you, of course," Pearl added.

"You don't need to pay," Lesia murmured. "I'd be happy to make them for you."

She looked appalled. "If not money, then you must take food. I insist."

"Well," Lesia said shyly, "I would like to buy some shells for the shotgun."

"We'll save you a trip to the store and give you those, along with some flour, some potatoes and a small jar of cooking oil," Pearl said. "How does that sound?"

"That's far too much."

The older woman shook her head. "Not for something this elaborate."

Mama shot Lesia a silencing look. "We would be very grateful," she said firmly.

The next morning at church, several other women expressed interest when Pearl showed off Lesia's belt. They had no time to make their own and theirs *never* turned out as nice. Would Lesia make one for them? By the time the church service was over, Pearl had taken orders for five belts at twenty cents apiece.

One dollar to weave five belts. It was enough to buy a piglet in spring. And more food!

Leaving church, Minnie sidled up to Lesia. "They feel sorry for you," she whispered. "That's why they're buying them."

In spite of the bitter cold, a wave of heat passed through Lesia. It wasn't true! The women had liked them. She couldn't wait to get away from Minnie's nastiness. Though Pearl had wanted them to stay much longer, Mama hadn't wanted to impose. She had insisted on leaving today. Thank goodness!

"They're ugly," Minnie continued. "Real bohunk stuff. I'm going to lose mine down the well as soon as I get it."

It was bad enough to hear Canadians call them bohunks, but to hear a Ukrainian say it was more than Lesia could stand.

"I can think of a better use for it." She forced a smile. Anyone looking would think they were having a pleasant conversation. "You could stuff it inside your mouth."

Minnie gasped. Lesia's smile turned genuine. "It would save everyone the pain of listening to you!" she concluded sweetly before hurrying towards Andrew's wagon.

For once she had gotten the best of Minnie Korol!

Chapter Seventeen

February 2, 1915

The Magus homestead

The sky was just beginning to brighten as Lesia crunched over the frozen ground towards the creek. The wind stung her cheeks, whipped her hair into fine strings around her face and sent tiny flecks of crystal snow onto her eyelids. Bozhe, it was cold! She couldn't wait for spring. For warmth. And birdsong.

Christmas and its festivities were a distant memory. Letters from the men were sporadic now, as though Papa and Ivan had given up and accepted their fate. Last night, when Lesia had dipped her hand into the sack of potatoes, she had touched bottom. The next time Andrew came by, she would give him the belt money for food.

In the meantime, they needed fresh meat. She had put it off as long as she could. It was time to hunt.

There was a rustle in a clump of bushes. Her heart thumped.

Fumbling, she reached for the shotgun, hoisted it to her shoulder and pointed. Was it a rabbit? Or a partridge? She stood still, breath held, eyes glued on softly swaying branches. Waiting.

Instead, the bush rustled and stopped.

It was moving with the wind!

She unclenched her hand and slowly lowered the shotgun. How foolish! Everything was moving in the wind. Her hair, the trees, the light dusting of snow that had fallen overnight.

Chagrined, she continued on her way. The water left in the creek at the end of summer had hardened into a thin slick of shiny ice. The only opening was the hole at the edge where Lesia had broken through to wash their clothes. It was here, Andrew had told her, that the animals would come, instinctively drawn to the creek for a drink.

She hoped he was right.

Leaning against a thin poplar, she thought over his instructions. Pull the hammer. Brace yourself. Line up the notches with your prey. And shoot.

How hard could it be?

She practised by picking out a twig in the distance and lining up the notches at each end of the barrel. As Andrew had explained, one shot would fire off a blast of small pellets. If she could hold the gun steady and keep her prey in sight, her chances were good. Excellent, in fact.

They'd better be. She had two shells with her. She was counting on getting something with each of them.

Steadying herself against the trunk of the tree, she pulled the hammer back and waited.

There! Near the base of that bush. A brown rabbit. Poised, still.

She hoisted the shotgun, lined up the notches, leaned forward and pulled the trigger.

BAAAAAAAAM. The kick sent her staggering backwards. She yelped in pain as her shoulder caught the edge of the tree and pellets rained through the air, peppering her skin.

Relieved that there was no one to witness her first embarrassing attempt, Lesia scrambled to her feet. She held the shotgun gingerly, not wanting to lose her last shell. The rabbit, of course, was long gone.

Both Andrew and Paul had told her to expect the painful kickback, but she hadn't expected it to be quite that strong.

Hunting was a lot harder than it looked.

She walked along the creek, past the site of the summer garden to the field that Andrew and the others had cleared. The sun was completely up now and the snow sparkled with tiny rainbow prisms as it rolled to the edge of the horizon. It was so blinding in its brightness that it made her eyes water.

Bozhe, the prairie was beautiful! Wide and open and free. And to think she had once found it ugly.

Moving quickly generated heat, something her shivering body craved. Lesia kept walking, eventually taking up another position in sight of the creek. She wished she could stamp some warmth into her feet, but sound or movement might scare away animals.

She didn't have to wait long. Soon one rabbit appeared, then another. She had to try!

Raising the shotgun, she lined up the notches, braced herself and pulled back the hammer with a stiff, frozen finger.

The rabbits bolted.

Lesia lowered the gun.

Two more rabbits quickly came into view. Then a third. She had to shoot. She couldn't take the cold much longer. This might be her last chance.

Taking a wide stance, she planted both feet firmly in the snow, raised the shotgun and lined up the biggest rabbit. Squeezing one eye shut, she reached for the trigger. She stiffened her arms and forced her frozen finger to move. *BAAAAAAAAAAAM!*

Lesia's feet were steady, but her upper body still couldn't handle the force of the kickback. When her right arm faltered, the gun slipped back and ploughed into her lip. She was going to have a bruise there tomorrow. Slowly she lowered the gun to her waist.

Two rabbits lay limp on the ground. Their blood oozed out of them, a crimson mat against the pure white snow.

Knees trembling, she hurried forward. Wide eyes stared up at her, sharp, black, innocent. But dead. She bent down to pick them up by their haunches. Thoughts of the prairie chicken filled her head. For a minute, Lesia was dizzy.

It didn't get any easier, this killing to eat.

Holding the two rabbits at arm's length, Lesia hurried back to the burdei. Blood stained the snow behind her like petals falling from a poppy.

Just as she emerged from the bushes, she saw the flash of Mama's skirt. One look at her mother's face and she knew something was wrong.

Mama pointed.

Lesia followed her finger.

There was a coyote. Standing near the hole where the chickens were kept, with feathers at its feet, blood around its muzzle and a look of satisfaction in its eyes.

"Noooooooooo!" Lesia lunged forward, flinging the gun over her shoulders with a strength she hadn't known she possessed.

The coyote turned and ran.

The woven cover to the chicken hole was feet away from where it was supposed to be. Girlie and Noisy were gone. Tears sprang to Lesia's eyes. "Oh, Mama, no! Those poor creatures . . . what will we tell Sonia . . . and Adam?" *What will we do without eggs this spring?*

"Hush now." Mama's eyes were soft, her voice gentle. "We'll figure something out."

"I shouldn't have put the chickens out this morning!" Her arms trembled and the rabbits jerked from side to side, their blood spraying. "It's cold and there are coyotes everywhere. I should have kept them inside." Bozhe, Bozhe! What had she done?

Mama took the rabbits with one hand and gave Lesia a hug with the other. "Where they could peck at Adam? I think not. As God ordains, so it shall be. The chickens are gone. There is nothing we can do. Now come. We have two rabbits to skin." Frowning, she reached out and gently touched the corner of Lesia's mouth. "And your lip to fix. It is badly cut."

The cold had frozen her mouth almost immediately after the gun had hit it. She reached up and wiped, only mildly surprised to find a smear of blood on her hand.

Life on the prairie, she decided bleakly as she followed Mama inside, was a bloody, unkind business.

⁂

The days blurred together, a kaleidoscope of blowing snow and freezing cold, of hunger that came and went, depending on Lesia's success with the shotgun. When the wind wasn't too fierce and the cold not so biting, she would go outside and hunt. Over the next three weeks, she caught four more rabbits and a half-frozen-to-death prairie chicken. Mama pounced on the meat with a frenzy bordering on madness. Nothing was wasted. The skin was dried and set aside. The meat was stretched into two meals, sometimes three. The carcass was boiled for soup.

Adam turned seven months old on March 10, and he was a living reminder of Slavko, the little brother they had buried in the homeland. Perhaps that's why Lesia's thoughts turned to Shuparka more and more during those long winter days when they were stuck inside. She and Ivan had been so sure leaving was the right thing to do. But if they'd stayed in Shuparka, they would all be together now. And they could go outside to visit the graves of their loved ones.

Eventually, Lesia saw signs that spring was coming. Daylight lasted a little longer each afternoon. The snow began to recede from the top of the burdei. The buds on the trees plumped out; the wild animals became more active. The skeps were hung out again and Lesia prayed nightly for bees.

One morning, when she returned to the burdei with a rabbit under her arm, she saw a horse and wagon in the clearing. The tall, black horse had a thick red blanket over its back. The fancy brown wagon had gold and red lettering on its side.

Her heart began to pound. Dear Lord, the Mounties had found out about the money she had sent to Master Stryk!

She hurried into the burdei and saw Mama standing beside a man wearing a dark fur coat and beaver hat. Sonia sat clutching Adam, her blue eyes wide with fear.

"This man," Mama said in swift Ukrainian, "he wants you to give up the gun. Pretend you do not understand."

Trembling, Lesia dropped the rabbit onto the floor. Praise God, it wasn't about the money!

She clutched the gun in her hand and wished she had left it outside or hidden it in the chicken hole, as she sometimes did. It was all she could do not to eye it guiltily. Instead she focused on the stranger. He had a pleasantly round face, but his eyes were a flat black, narrow and suspicious.

"Yes?" she asked in English.

"You understand English?" His black eyes took on some warmth; he looked almost eager. "You speak it?"

Her understanding was growing, but her English-speaking skills were still weak. "Some," she admitted.

He pointed to the gun. "Under the War Measures Act, you are not allowed to have that."

She understood perfectly well but she pretended not to. "Ya," she gave him a wide, dumb smile. "Makes good hunting, ya?"

"You cannot have the gun," he said again. He held out his hand. "Give it to me."

She feigned confusion. "You want food?" She turned to fetch the rabbit, wondering if she dared make a dash for the chicken hole.

"No!" He held up a hand to stop her. "You cannot have the gun," he explained again. "You are enemies of the state and, as such, you must not have a gun."

Mama bit her lower lip and gave Lesia the tiniest shake of her head. *Don't give up,* she seemed to be saying.

Lesia's frown was genuine. *Enemies.* She knew that word. "Not enemies." Her palm was damp where she clutched the gun. The gun she had been so scared to use. The gun that had prevented them from starving to death.

He reached into his pocket. "This promissory note explains everything. When the war is over, you can reclaim it."

Lesia wouldn't take the paper. She stepped backwards. "Everybody has guns," she said haltingly.

"Not everybody." The man's eyes narrowed even further. "And we have had complaints," he said. "People say you've handled the gun carelessly."

Suddenly Lesia knew. Her neighbours had reported her.

"Here." He leaned forward and jabbed the corner of the note towards her free hand.

She jerked away and went to stand beside Sonia and Adam. "Without meat . . ." she struggled to find the right words, "the children, they will . . . starve," she concluded softly.

Tiny beads of perspiration appeared on the man's forehead. He pulled out a white handkerchief and dabbed at his hairline.

"There are food lines in Winnipeg." He refused to look at the children. "They can help."

"Baah!" Lesia's anger exploded and she began babbling in Ukrainian. "Winnipeg is a two-day walk. That's too far in this cold! We are not enemies of the state. We work hard to clear the land. To feed our families. What do you do? You lock our men away. And now you want to take away our means of survival?" She clutched the gun to her chest and glared defiantly at the stranger. "No!"

His full lips twisted into an angry sneer. "Then I have no choice but to take you with me." His face lost some of its pleasant roundness; his jaw jutted forward. He stepped towards her.

Mama cried out. Sonia began to wail.

Take you with me. Lesia knew those words. A chill crept down her spine. He wouldn't take her away! Would he? She looked into his eyes and saw the answer. He would.

Defeated, she held out the shotgun."Why do you hate us so much?" she whispered. "Why?"

The man didn't answer. Instead, he snatched the shotgun from her hand, threw the promissory note at her feet and bolted for the door.

Lesia was cold with shock. "I'm sorry, Mama."

Mama's eyes glistened with unshed tears. "You did the right thing. We couldn't—" Her voice trembled. She pressed her lips together and reached for her. "We could not survive without you. And I could not bear to have them take another of my family away."

Lesia crumpled into Mama's arms.

⁂

The wind was fierce that afternoon when Lesia went outside to lay the traps. It whistled through the trees, whipped at her skirt and pushed her sideways. She didn't care. She stomped angrily over the prairie with her head bowed against the gusts and the traps clutched firmly in her arms.

There was a rock in her path; roughly she kicked it away. This land—the land she had yearned for—was the cause of all her trouble. She laid the traps quickly, anxious to get the job done and return to Mama and the others. She put the last trap down by the garden and turned to go.

That's when she saw it.

One of the bee skeps was lying on the ground. A tree branch had come down, taking the skep with it. Lesia pried it loose. It was badly crushed on one side.

Bozhe, what next?

Clutching the skep in her hands, Lesia cursed loud and long.

She cursed the wind and the climate. She cursed the soil for being so hard and heavy. She cursed the man who had taken the gun for being so cruel. She cursed the English Canadians for being so hateful.

And she cursed herself for daring to dream.

The sun does not always shine. But if your effort is true, the rewards will be sweet. It was like Baba was whispering in her ear.

Tears gathered behind her eyes. She had been so sure that Baba had been right. So trusting of what the beloved woman had told her the day she'd left Shuparka.

The flower is not always open, but if your effort is honest and true, just like the bees, your rewards will be sweet.

Baba had been wrong!

Lesia's throat closed; her tears began to fall. She sank to her knees. The broken bee skep didn't matter any more. The bees hadn't come. Life didn't always yield sweet rewards, even if the effort was honest and true.

The wind sent a flurry of snow into her face. Its shocking iciness brought the truth home to Lesia. The land of her dreams was a nightmare. She hadn't bettered herself here. She never would.

Wiping the snow from her eyes, she stared across the prairie.

They had been so wrong to come here. Only Mama had been right. She had wanted to stay behind. Well, Mama would be happy now. Because they were going home to Shuparka. One way or another, they were leaving this frozen land of Hell.

Lesia pulled herself up, tucked the damaged skep under her arm and made her way through the howling wind to the burdei. Shuparka wasn't perfect, but it was better than Canada. There, at least, the plum trees produced fruit in spring and the winters weren't so harsh. There, the language was familiar. True, there was Michal Stryk and the rest of the nobility, but what was that compared to the hate of an entire country? Nothing at all.

To go back home, however, they needed money.

Lots of it.

There was only one thing left to do.

Chapter Eighteen

The shotgun was gone, the bee skep was ruined, and Baba had been wrong.

I cried. Oh, how I cried.

You might think it is silly to become despondent over something my baba said. What did she know, an old woman living all her life in a little village?

Well, I am old now, and I know that old women see things the rest of the world does not. Even then I knew Baba was wise. She saw beyond the ordinary. She saw . . . how do you say in English? The extraordinary.

When I realized Baba had been wrong, the last of my hope died.

I dreamed of Shuparka the way a drowning man dreams of an arm coming out of the sea.

Mama said no. Spring was coming, she said. The traps would bring food. She would fix the skep. But then Paul was taken, locked up for travelling without his papers. Mama was shattered.

It was time to go back, she said. It was time.

March 31, 1915

Winnipeg, Manitoba

"I forbid it!" The words came out in a shout. Furious, Andrew scowled down at her.

How *dare* he? Defiantly, Lesia stared back at him. "You have no right to forbid me to do anything. You are not my father. Or my brother." *Or my husband*, she added silently as she clutched Baba's precious box and Geedo's Bible. "I am fifteen. I have travelled halfway around the world. I can certainly go into a pawnshop by myself."

Some people were staring; others were hurrying down the street, pretending not to hear. An old woman clutched a heavily embroidered shawl with thick, stubby fingers. She stopped beside Lesia. "Are you all right?" she asked in familiar Ukrainian. Her world-weary brown eyes peered kindly into Lesia's face. "Do you need help?"

She reminded Lesia of Baba. Of the sacrifice she was about to make. Before she could answer, a man rushed up, grabbed the old woman by the arm and hurried her away.

"If you had told me what you planned to do, I never would have agreed to accompany you to Winnipeg."

"I would have come on my own, then," Lesia said calmly.

She was more than capable of taking the train from Hazelridge to Winnipeg. She had even managed to save the forty-cent train fare out of her belt money.

Andrew glared at the bounty she held in her arms. "You're a foolish woman, putting a price on priceless family heirlooms."

"The only foolish thing would be staying in this country one second longer than I have to."

A red flush of heat crept up his neck. "Now you are talking like a *crazy* woman!"

Lesia had the ridiculous but overwhelming urge to laugh. She had never seen Andrew so worked up. Never even suspected he was capable of it. But if he thought going to the pawnshop was crazy, just wait until he learned about her plans to go to the internment camp to buy Papa's and Ivan's release. It meant catching a late train to Brandon, and sleeping in the train station until she could catch a train home the next morning.

"Lesia, please, be reasonable." Andrew's tone was more conciliatory now. "Let's talk about this."

"No." Lesia turned and began to walk. The pawnshop was up ahead and across the street. Its large red sign was cheerful against the grey glumness of the midday sky. Now that it was the end of March, the snow was beginning to melt. It wasn't as noticeable in the country, but here in the city, lumps of dirty snow pooled on the road and at the edges of the sidewalk.

She heard footsteps behind her. Andrew, no doubt. She wouldn't turn around to check. Instead, she walked steadily forward, her fingers caressing the worn leather of the Bible as she went.

Hold this Bible close and you hold me close. It will comfort you . . . and help you keep the faith.

She remembered Geedo, with his shoulders poking through his worn jacket and the candlelight playing on the walls as he'd bent over the pages of the Holy Book.

With her other hand, she traced the intricate designs on the box. She remembered Baba carefully unwrapping it from layers and layers of rags and sheepskin so she could polish it with a little bit of oil every Christmas.

When she stopped at the intersection, Lesia glanced casually back to see if Andrew was close. He was standing where she had left him, watching her.

She looked away. Her finger found a flower. Slowly she followed the overlapping petals until she reached the tiny bee nestled at its core. It reminded her of Baba's words. *Remember always the bees. They work long and they work hard . . . but how sweet their reward.*

Her eyes filled with tears. They'd worked long and hard and nothing had come of it. They desperately needed money.

It won't always be easy for you. The flower is not always open.

She didn't want easy. She wanted possibilities. There were no possibilities in Canada, Lesia reminded herself as she crossed the road. Not unless you counted internment, discrimination and enough cold weather to freeze people's hearts.

She wiped her tears, took a deep breath and stopped in front of the pawnshop. Suddenly afraid, she resisted the urge to look back at Andrew. Would they take her things? Scoff at her belts? Jeer at the workmanship of the box?

There was only one way to find out.

A tinkling bell announced her entry. The room was warm, the lighting dim, and the air was rich with the smell of leather and tobacco and the burnt-sugar candies favoured by old Master Stryk. A comforting smell, Lesia thought, moving past tables, an ornate brass bed and a huge, rounded cabinet filled with more silver and glass than she'd ever seen in one place before.

"Yes?" A short, heavy-set man stood behind the counter, fiddling with the tiny pieces of a gold pocket watch.

Lesia hesitated. The sign on the door was in English. While her English was improving, it was still poor. "You buy?" She held out her weaving first.

His round, flushed face moved from the watch to her hand. "Nope." He shook his head.

Buy? Was it *buy?* No. That wasn't the word Wasyl had used.

Lesia tried again. "You pawn?" She thrust the largest and most colourful belt under his nose. "Here."

This time he looked right at her. Muddy brown eyes peered out from underneath bushy grey eyebrows. Tiny red veins littered chipmunk cheeks. His bulbous nose wrinkled in distaste. "Lady, look around." He made a grand, sweeping gesture with one arm. "Does it look like I pawn bohunk material in here?" He shook his head again. "No value. No market." He picked up the pocket watch.

No. That she understood. And *bohunk*. She understood that all too well. Indignation flooded through her. Bozhe, these Canadians were a nasty, insulting lot. She couldn't *wait* to return to Shuparka. At least there she knew the language and the insults. She could give them back as good as she got!

She shoved the belt into her pocket and resisted the urge to stomp out to the street. Swallowing her pride, she pulled Geedo's Bible and Baba's box from behind her back. "These, then."

Holding her breath, she watched the man glance casually from his watch to Lesia's hand. His eyes lingered on the cherrywood box. They narrowed. The pocket watch slipped to the counter. He reached out with calloused, dirty hands. Bozhe! She couldn't bear the thought of him touching the box, never mind keeping it in his store.

"Nice," he said approvingly.

"This too." Lesia pressed the Bible towards him. He thumbed through it just long enough to note the Ukrainian characters. "Not English." He handed it back.

"Ukrainian." She shoved it back at him.

He paid no attention. Both hands were on the box now. He held it up to the dim light, looked at the bottom, checked the hinges, fingered the worn lining. His eyes gleamed with interest. "Five bucks," he said with a smack of his lips.

"What?" Lesia was horrified. She must have misunderstood.

"I'll buy it. No pawn. Five bucks." He held up five fingers. "This is a bohunk box. Nice work, but still bohunk. Some farmer might want it to keep records and things in." He still had his hands on it, as though it already belonged to him.

"Not enough." Lesia shook her head. "I need more." Twenty times more, at least.

"Five bucks is all. Buy lots of potatoes with five bucks. Make lots of pyrohy. Feed all those mouths." He laughed cruelly.

Five dollars. A pittance. *Foolish woman, putting a price on priceless family heirlooms.* Andrew had been right. Hot tears gathered behind her eyes. But if he took both . . .

She pushed Geedo's Bible forward. "This too." Together, they would fetch more money.

He didn't look at the Bible, didn't even touch it. "No." He

was still holding the box with a proprietary air, still tracing the pattern with his grimy fingers.

Only five dollars? It wouldn't cover train fare to Brandon, and it certainly wasn't enough to buy Papa's and Ivan's release. Tears pushed relentlessly behind her eyes. Five dollars was hardly even a start on their passage home.

Furiously, Lesia blinked away her tears. She wouldn't give up Baba's box for five dollars! She couldn't. Quickly, before she had time to think, she snatched the box from his fingers. "No."

"Hey." He lunged over the counter and tried to grab it back. When Lesia held it out of reach, he let loose with a stream of words she had heard before. Nasty, insulting words about Ukrainians and Poles and Germans. The usual shame overwhelmed her. *After today*, she vowed, *I will stay on our land and have nothing more to do with the English until I can buy our passage home.* She wouldn't even go to the internment camp. She wouldn't have enough money to justify the risk, and she couldn't take any more shame.

But then she was struck by a thought that chased some of her shame away. The man wanted the box. Really, really wanted it. Suddenly, Lesia felt powerful, courageous. "You take this." She held up the Bible. "And this." She pulled the biggest belt from her pocket. "You give me twenty dollars. And then you can have the box."

"Twenty dollars?" The man's face turned even redder. His nose stuck out like a scorched plum. "You are a thief. How dare you come into my store and try to rob me! You bohunks don't belong here. Why don't you go back to where you came from?"

He cursed, he insulted, he waved his fist. Lesia just stood there and waited. She would leave with nothing before she took five dollars for Baba's box. It had cost them almost three hundred Canadian dollars to come to Canada. It was going to cost them that to go back. Saving would take a long time. And they had to eat in the meantime.

If the man's yelling was any indication, he wanted the box. Very badly.

"Fifteen dollars," he finally said with a sneer.

Lesia pressed her lips together. "Twenty." She held the Bible and the belt in one hand. "For this and this." She waved the box with the other. "And this."

He let loose with another stream of curses. His face got even redder. Lesia could see a vein pulsing in his temple. What if he died right in front of her? She'd rush for the door, pretend she'd never seen him before.

"Eighteen," he roared. "That's all!"

The box alone was worth far more. But Lesia knew he wouldn't give her twenty. That would be letting her win. And he wasn't about to let a Ukrainian win. It was eighteen or nothing.

Reluctantly she nodded. "Eighteen," she repeated.

He reached into his pocket, quickly counted out some bills and slapped them onto the counter. "Now give me the box," he snapped. "And that Ukrainian holy book."

She laid the belt on the counter first.

"Ugly trash." He pushed it back to her. "Couldn't give it away. Keep it."

Just another insult, Lesia thought dully, shoving the belt back into her pocket.

He eyed the box greedily, hungrily. "Come on. Haven't got all day."

Baba held these. Loved these. Geedo, too. Lesia hugged them close for one last minute. Then slowly, reluctantly, she unfurled her arms and relinquished her last physical ties to her grandparents. Sadly, she walked back through the door of the pawnshop to the street.

She was eighteen dollars richer. But Geedo's precious Bible and Baba's beloved box were gone. Her dream of being worthy and respected and rich in the land of milk and honey was over. And Lesia's heart was broken.

Chapter Nineteen

"There's mail for you." Andrew threw a bale of hay into the back of the wagon and then reached into his pocket and handed her a letter. "Are you sure you don't want to come into the store and look around?"

Lesia shook her head.

He opened his mouth and then shut it again. Wordlessly, he turned and headed back inside for the last of her supplies.

All the fight seemed to have drained out of Andrew in Winnipeg. Just as he had accepted Lesia's silence on the train leaving Winnipeg, he had accepted the nine dollars she'd handed him when they'd arrived back in Hazelridge. She had asked him to stop at the store, and, when she had rattled off the list of things they would need for the next six months, he hadn't even blinked.

She didn't want to set foot in another store. She didn't want to deal with the English until it was time to buy their passage home. She didn't even want to spend the night at Paul's farm, as Andrew had suggested. She just wanted to be alone.

She opened the envelope and removed a single sheet of paper.

Dear Lesia, Ivan had written. *Things are changing rapidly in this place. Men are being released on parole to factories that are short of labour because of the war. They are paying almost nothing and the men are still slaves, but they are paid slaves. Perhaps that is the best we can wish for at this time. Paul is here, as you may know. He is convinced it is all a mistake and he will be released soon. We all think that when we first come in. We had news of the homeland last week. Master Stryk is dead. No doubt his son, Michal, is in charge now. Your loving brother, Ivan.*

After tucking the letter away, Lesia stared into the late-afternoon sky. Thick, grey snow clouds rolled together, like a crowd of angry people. The wind pushed relentlessly against her shoulders; she pulled her tattered shawl tight and slid low on the seat. Hard to believe it was almost April.

Hard to believe she had gone halfway around the world chasing a dream, only to fail.

Another pair of chickens scratched in the box behind her, and Lesia sighed. They would have eggs soon . . . and full bellies for a little while. In another month or so, she would put in the garden. It was going to take them a long time to save for the passage home, a year, maybe longer.

A low, deep rumble came from the side of the wagon. It sounded like a cross between a bleat and a moo. Startled, Lesia's eyes flew open. "What is *that*?"

Andrew held a brown parcel in his left hand and a piece of frayed old rope in his right. At the end of it was a spotted brown-and-white animal. He grinned proudly. "A cow."

A young cow with the biggest, saddest brown eyes she had ever seen, three sorry-looking teats hanging from its belly, a mashed-up ear and a crooked nose.

"I didn't know you needed another cow," Lesia said.

"I don't. Take this, would you? It's the last of your stuff." After Lesia took the package and stored it away, Andrew swatted the cow on the behind. "Git." When the animal wouldn't budge, he crouched down, scooped it into his arms and hoisted it into the wagon with a grunt.

Lesia yelped as the animal immediately clambered onto the seat and practically into her lap.

"Grab it and hold on!" Andrew ordered. "It's going to try and get out the other side."

Gasping in pain as the cow's hoof stood on her stomach, Lesia clutched the rope and shoved the animal off. Not only was it heavy, it smelled terrible. The cow gave her an indignant stare before making its strange moo-bleat sound. It tottered on the seat beside them and then, seeing an opening, it bolted for the back of the wagon.

Andrew was too fast. With one large hand, he pulled the animal back before climbing into his seat. "Lie down," he ordered.

In spite of her glum mood, Lesia giggled. "It's not a dog. I don't think it takes orders. Besides, it *should* go into the back."

"It sits up here with us, otherwise it'll escape."

The animal nuzzled Lesia's ear with its cold nose. She giggled again. It made its strange moo sound once more and this time Lesia laughed. Poor, gangly thing.

"Hold on to the rope," Andrew ordered as the wagon began to move. Snow was starting to fall. "We're in for a storm, and I want to be home before it starts. Don't want to stop and chase a cow."

After a little while, the cow settled between them. Lesia waited for Andrew to speak, but he was silent. Lesia knew he was waiting for her to say something.

"I made eighteen dollars." The snow was starting to cling to her skirt. She brushed it away. "I have nine dollars for the Shuparka fund. It's a start."

"Uh huh."

Well. She was hoping for a bit more of a reaction. "In Winnipeg, you called me a crazy woman. Now all you can say is 'Uh huh'?"

"You can save all the money you want," Andrew said, "but you can't go back. Not now."

"Of course I can," Lesia countered with a flash of annoyance. "I can do anything I put my mind to."

"And what about Adam?"

She frowned. "What about Adam? He goes too, of course."

Andrew gave her a quick glance before turning his attention back to the road. "He was born here. Adam's a Canadian. He won't be accepted in the homeland. Even after the war, people will remember Canada was against them. What are you going to do?" he asked softly. "Leave little Adam behind?"

Adam's a Canadian. The words hung in the space between

them. He couldn't go to Ukraine. Not now. Not later. And they couldn't leave him behind. It was unthinkable.

What were they going to do?

"I never would have taken you for a quitter," Andrew added.

"I'm no quitter!" Lesia retorted indignantly. "Ivan and I came to Canada because we thought we would be welcome. Like Pearl said, we have watered this land with our own blood, sweat and tears. All I want in return is respect and acceptance. A peaceful life. Some warmth and some food. I just want to belong," she admitted. "Even in Shuparka I'm not an enemy alien." Adam was a Canadian. They couldn't go home.

The snow was getting heavier. It was harder to see the road ahead. A thin white dusting covered the oxen. "Belonging takes time," Andrew said. "I've been here thirteen years and I still don't belong. Not like the Irish and the Scottish do. But remember, we've been outsiders in our own land for centuries. We still are. Give Canada a chance."

How could Andrew be so accepting? "Don't you hear what people call us?" Lesia demanded hotly. "The things they say about us?"

"Canadians aren't all bad. They don't all say those things."

"Most do," she retorted quickly.

Mutely, Andrew nodded.

"How do you stand it?"

"It's ignorance, Lesia. And I won't let ignorance make me bitter. There are worse things in life than being hated, believe me." He paused and Lesia knew that he was thinking of his dead wife. "Besides," he added, "Canada offers hope. We have to hold on to that."

"How can you say that when they've imprisoned innocent men? And now taken Paul into the camp?"

One of the oxen chose that moment to wander left. Andrew struggled for control. It still amazed Lesia that he had taught the animals to pull the wagon like a team of horses; most people walked beside their oxen.

Once the animal was in line, Andrew said, "I'm not happy about it, but what can I do? Paul shouldn't have been travelling without his papers. He knows the law."

"What will happen to his farm? To Pearl and the children?"

Even in profile, Lesia could see Andrew's lips pressed thin. "I'll do what I can. Wasyl is still around too. He's moving from farm to farm, staying two steps ahead of the authorities. He'll help. So will the others." He paused and shot Lesia a quick glance. "But Paul will be released. So will your Papa and Ivan." His blue eyes gleamed with conviction. "We have to get through the war. We have to trust the Canadians to do the right thing."

"I'm fresh out of trust," Lesia muttered. She thought of the sneering pawnshop owner, the greedy neighbour who had dammed up the creek, the unfriendliness of the storekeeper. Was that what she had to look forward to for the rest of her life? Not if she could help it. "I'll stay on our land," she vowed. "I'll give my heart to the prairie. But I'll have nothing more to do with the English."

"Huh." Andrew flicked the reins. The oxen picked up speed. "It's going to be hard to sell your butter with that attitude."

At first she didn't understand. "What butter?"

He looked at the cow and then at her.

Horrified, Lesia's eyes widened. "You didn't!"

"I did."

"But . . . but . . . !" She couldn't stop sputtering.

"Bought and paid for with your own money." He gestured with his thumb to the back of the wagon. "There should be enough food to keep her fed until the grass starts to grow. There's a butter churn too. You'll need it."

"A churn?" Her voice was shrill enough to cause the cow to make its moo-bleat sound again. "I gave you nine dollars. You didn't have enough for a churn and chickens and food and supplies *and* a cow." She stared at the creature. She'd never seen anything so ugly in her life.

"They were taking her to the slaughterhouse tomorrow." Andrew reached over and scratched the animal's ear.

She wouldn't let herself feel sorry. She wouldn't even look at those big, brown eyes. "Why?"

"She went into labour two months early. The calf died. Her milk's never really come in. She's skittish and frail. Owner's convinced she'll be a lousy milker, but I'm not so sure." Andrew's eyes narrowed. "He has a reputation of being hard on animals. The better cows are treated, the better they milk."

"How much did she cost?"

"Six dollars."

She didn't believe him. Milking cows fetched thirty or forty dollars. Even a three-teated cow had to be worth at least twenty. "I owe you money. Tell me how much."

"Make me some butter and we'll call it even."

She rolled her eyes. Andrew needed butter like she needed more insults. The man was impossible. But she couldn't take more of his charity. She finally understood how Papa felt. When you had nothing and no hope of earning respect, looking after yourself was the only source of pride left.

"You'll have to take her," she said stiffly. "I don't have time to look after a cow."

Andrew found that especially amusing. After he stopped laughing, he said, "I didn't realize a cow took that much time."

Lesia looked at the cow. The cow looked at her.

She had begged Papa for a cow. But not, she thought critically, a three-teated one with a mashed-in ear and a crooked nose. Not a cow that everyone would laugh at.

The animal studied her with sad, wistful brown eyes.

Lesia felt herself weakening. Fresh milk would be wonderful for Sonia and Adam. That and the butter would bring in some much-needed extra money.

"I'll look after her, but Mama will have to sell the butter and the cream," she told him. "I'm not going to town again."

"I'm sure you'll figure something out," Andrew said cheerfully.

Wet snow was gathering in the hollows on the ground. The animals would have to go inside tonight, Lesia thought. Three chickens, four people and a scrawny, three-teated cow all crammed into the burdei. It was going to be unbearably crowded.

"Oh, by the way," Andrew said. "I've named her."

Lesia was silent.

"Her name's Faith."

Faith. Baba had told her to hold the Bible close and it would help her keep the faith. The Bible was gone.

But Faith, with her loving, trusting, big brown eyes, was right beside her.

Chapter Twenty

May 9, 1915

Beausejour, Manitoba

Lesia was going to market. And she was going to be sick.

But her only sickness was cowardice. She didn't want to face the Canadians.

You don't belong here. You're a dirty peasant. A worthless servant. They were words she had travelled halfway around the world to get away from. Words that kept coming back to haunt her.

She'd had enough derision, enough scorn, to last a lifetime. She couldn't go to market.

Yet she *was* going.

All because of Faith. With a little love and care, the cow had turned into an incredible milker, more than making up for the missing teat. Her milk was fresh, rich and tasted faintly of prairie grass and clover. But no matter how much they cooked with it, they couldn't use it all. And Lesia couldn't bear to see the extra go to waste.

Andrew's wagon bounced with the ruts in the road. Now that it was May, the farmers had changed from sled runners to wheels. The snow was almost gone, dissolving into grey lumps, pooling and running into rivers and creeks and sloughs.

The drier fields had been ploughed and readied for planting. When the wind blew, the soil swirled into dancing brown clouds. Sometimes the air was so thick with dust that Lesia couldn't see the tops of the trees.

Today, however, she could see everything: trees, fields and the high-water line of the Brokenhead River shimmering in the morning sun as they pulled into town.

Beausejour was crowded with other wagons and horses, people on foot, groups of children laughing and playing. The joyful atmosphere reminded Lesia of some of the markets she used to go to back home.

It reminded her all over again that she didn't belong in Canada.

Andrew parked in a field. The ground rolled on endlessly, waves of earth coming to life after winter's deep freeze. The river was so close she could see the silver sheen of the water as it rippled downstream. A nearby tamarack tree overflowed with velvety red rosettes, and in the distance, a small cluster of crabapple trees frothed with blushing pink blooms.

How could I ever have thought the prairie was ugly? Lesia wondered as she got out of the wagon. *It has its own special beauty.*

Women in colourful Ukrainian clothing were setting up tables. Men rushed back and forth carrying boxes of goods to sell. Maybe the English wouldn't be here, she thought hopefully. Maybe it would just be Ukrainians and Poles. And other immigrants like them.

"Lesia!" Pearl waved.

After exchanging hugs and news, Lesia asked about Paul. The older woman just shook her head and changed the subject. "We have two tables," she told Lesia. "I'm at one and Minnie is selling bread at the other one." She motioned her daughter forward. "There's room on her table for you."

"Hello." Minnie gave her a small half smile.

English Canadians weren't the only hostile ones, Lesia reminded herself as she gave the girl a curt nod. She wished she had the nerve to ask Pearl to trade places. Her table was covered with rhubarb, early spring greens and sparkling jars of preserves. Why couldn't Minnie's bread go there?

"I'm off," Andrew called.

A prick of horror skittered down her back. He wasn't going to *leave* her here, was he? "Where are you going?"

"I have an errand to run," he said, "and I'm not sure I'll be back before dark. I told your mama that you might spend the night with Pearl."

Ignoring Minnie's disdainful sniff, Lesia watched Andrew walk away until he was a small, dark speck at the edge of the field. Then she got to work setting up her goods in time for the market to open. A slight breeze lifted the edge of her skirt and carried with it the smell of sweet bread, spring greens and her own fresh butter. She checked her wooden box again. The small blocks were still firm and cold. Andrew had come up with the idea of laying ice on the bottom of the box, followed by her eggs and then the butter.

The breeze from the river was nice on the back of her neck,

Lesia thought as she glanced idly around. Squinting at a nearby sign, she slowly sounded out the English letters. D-A-N-G-E-R.

Danger! The sign had been newly painted, and Lesia guessed that it warned of the rising water from the spring runoff.

Turning to Minnie, she pointed out the sign.

Minnie's mouth fell open. "You can read that?"

Lesia swallowed her grin. "I've been reading English for months." Weeks was more like it, but pride allowed her to stretch the truth.

The other girl looked impressed. "You're not so dumb after all."

This time she did grin. Trust Minnie to offer a compliment and an insult in the same breath. "Ukrainians, like *us*, are smart people," she said.

Minnie lowered her eyes.

When the market opened, they weren't busy like some of the other tables. At first, Lesia didn't mind. But then she began to feel invisible. People strolled by, chattering with each other, glancing at the tables as they walked. Stopping at some of them. But not at hers.

Andrew had said Pearl's bread was sure to sell out. Minnie had sold one loaf, or was it two? And even then she'd had to haggle over the price. How humiliating. Lesia hadn't sold one bit of butter. Or any eggs.

A little girl with black ringlets spun in a crazy circle just yards away from Lesia's table. Her pink-and-yellow dress twirled and rippled with the movement. It was the same child from the store in Hazelridge! The one whose hand had been smashed with the scale.

Where were her parents?

Lesia couldn't see them. Content to spin and twist and dance with the wind, the little girl didn't seem to mind.

How wonderful to be that young and carefree, Lesia thought.

A tall woman with thin, pinched lips stopped in front of Lesia. "How much is the butter?" she asked in a nasally voice. A brown-suited man clutched her elbow.

"Eighteen cents a pound." Lesia tried to erase any thread of eagerness from her voice.

The man nodded kindly but the woman tossed her head. "Too cheap," she proclaimed with a curl of her lips. "It's probably sour."

The man roared with laughter. Slowly they sauntered away.

Lesia stared at the ground until she felt the flush of heat fade from her face. Beside her, even Minnie looked embarrassed.

"It's because of Papa," the other girl said in a low, trembling voice. "They know he was taken away. That's why they won't buy our things." She wouldn't meet Lesia's eyes.

Was it true, or was there another reason? It didn't really matter. Lesia could tell by the defeated slump of Minnie's shoulders that Paul's internment had hit her hard. It couldn't be easy for her. But life *wasn't* easy. Maybe Minnie was finally figuring that out.

"We all have our crosses to bear," Lesia said, glancing away from Minnie towards the river.

There was that little girl again. Such a pretty little thing in her pink-and-yellow dress. Skipping back and forth behind a group of adults. Closer and closer to the white "Danger" sign. Surely one of them would watch her. The river was so high. It was overflowing its banks in places. She could fall in.

It's not your business.

It was a long time before anyone stopped at their table again. When they did, Lesia upped her price by two cents. "And it's good with the bread." She gestured to the loaves Minnie had proudly displayed.

"Too much." They waved vaguely over their shoulder. "It's cheaper over there."

"I also have eggs," she said. "Very fresh."

But the people were gone.

Lesia could feel Minnie's eyes studying her. She waited for the girl to insult her, to say something about her pathetic attempt to sell the butter and promote the bread. But Minnie was quiet.

Nervously, Lesia bent down and checked the butter. Was it melting? The sun was climbing; soon it would be midday, and the heat would intensify. But Andrew's packing job was holding up nicely.

The market was crowded now, full of people greeting friends and exchanging gossip, searching out the freshest milk and the tastiest bread. They still didn't seem interested in Pearl's bread. Or anything Lesia had to offer. Every once in a while, Lesia caught a glimpse of the little girl with the black ringlets. She was getting closer and closer to the edge of the riverbank.

It wasn't her business. Besides, when she had tried to help at the store, it hadn't been appreciated.

The young child laughed as she chased after a black-and-white butterfly. Had she ever been that carefree? If so, Lesia couldn't remember when.

The girl was getting closer and closer to the water. Bozhe! What if no one stopped her and she fell in?

She wouldn't. Lesia fought back her anxiety and turned away. She smiled at a passing group of people. They glanced at her eggs, slowed. But then the younger boy nudged his mother, pointed out larger eggs on a nearby table, and they moved on.

The little girl . . . where was the little girl? Lesia's heart lurched when she turned and couldn't find her. Ah, there she was, down the way, still laughing and chasing after the butterfly.

The adults were paying no attention.

She should stop her. Or say something. Her heart told her it was the right thing to do. But her head told her it wasn't her business. Surely her parents could read the "Danger" sign. She was a Ukrainian peasant. And hated by these people. Speaking up would only invite humiliation. She'd had enough of that to last a lifetime. She'd just stop looking at the child, that's what she'd do.

Restlessly she tapped her fingers on the edge of the table. The sun was high in the sky. Her stomach growled. It was almost lunchtime. Lesia wondered if she could trade Minnie some butter for a chunk of bread.

Involuntarily, her eyes floated back to the edge of the riverbank. The girl was still there.

And then, in a flash of pink and yellow, the child was gone.

There was no scream. No thumping fall. No rustle of fabric. Just there one minute and over the edge the next.

Lesia jumped up and craned her neck. She couldn't see a thing! There were people in the way.

"What is it?" Minnie asked.

Wildly, her eyes searched up and down the riverbank. There was no sign of her. Maybe she was with her parents. Heart pounding, Lesia turned and scanned the crowd.

No little girl.

Bozhe! She *couldn't* get involved. She was a useless, worthless peasant. People would be angry. They would misunderstand. She would be questioned. Maybe even taken away.

"What is it?" Minnie asked again.

"A girl," Lesia murmured, beads of sweat breaking out on her forehead. "I can't see her."

Suddenly the truth swept over her like a blast of wind, lifting away her doubts and insecurities like soil swirling up on the prairie. She wasn't worthless or useless or stupid. She wasn't dirty or scrawny, a liar or a thief. She was Lesia Magus, beloved daughter, beloved sister. Keeper of traditions, steward of the land.

She was a Ukrainian with a clear sense of right and wrong.

And not saving the girl would be wrong. No matter what other people thought.

"Watch my things." As she ran to the river, Baba's words echoed through her mind. *In the eyes of God, we are all equal. Peasants and landowners. Ukrainians and Canadians.*

Lesia could see the child now. Flailing arms . . . a tangle of pink and yellow . . . long black ringlets . . . the current already carrying her away. Lesia threw down her shawl and jumped into the water.

Bozhe! It was like liquid ice, filling her lungs and taking her breath away. The water pulled on her skirt, filled Papa's boots and weighed her down. It had been years since she'd been swimming, and that had been in a still pond. This was a river swollen with the spring melt, a river with currents that were moving, shifting and rolling her downstream.

Lesia fought with all her strength. Slowly, she neared the girl. Eventually her fingers clutched the collar of her dress. She pulled. The child came up sputtering and sobbing, her brown eyes wide with fear.

"Hold on to my neck," Lesia yelled.

The child didn't understand Ukrainian. Flailing, she pushed on Lesia's shoulders. They both went under the water. Surfacing again, Lesia struggled to place the child's arms just so. She seemed to understand. Finally, she was secure. With one arm around the child, Lesia used her other arm to fight her way back to shore.

Back to the crowd that had gathered on the riverbank.

Two men rushed into the water. Lesia recognized the child's father, Jack Scott, from the general store. He seized the little girl and hugged her to his chest, giving Lesia only the briefest of glances. The second man clutched Lesia's arms and pulled her to the water's edge. She stood there, cold and dripping, her clothes plastered to her body like clay on the outdoor oven.

"Are you all right?" The man spoke English.

Lesia didn't know what he was saying. Involuntarily, her teeth began to chatter. She was so cold.

Suddenly a dozen people surrounded her. Women were pulling off her clothes, men were shouting words Lesia didn't understand. Someone was towelling off her hair; another person was spooning luscious hot soup into her mouth.

"Great courage."

"A brave thing you did, saving Amy Scott."

"You should have called for help."

"You both could have drowned."

The words swirled and flowed and rolled and dipped . . . like the dust that floated on the air . . . the current that had tried to carry her downstream . . . the very prairie itself. Lesia heard everything and nothing. Nothing but the child.

The child. Little Amy Scott. Lesia had saved her. And that was all that mattered.

Later, when she was back at her table, warm and dry in borrowed clothes with a bowl of soup in her belly, people were still coming up to her table, shaking her hand, offering thanks.

"Tell them you'd rather have their money than their thanks," Minnie muttered disgustedly when another old man shook Lesia's hand. "All old Jack Scott did was glare at you. You saved his daughter. He's treating you like something on his boots."

"I don't care." She didn't need Jack Scott's approval any more. She had the approval of someone far more important. Herself. "I would like to sell my butter, though." Brooding, she studied her box. She hadn't sold one bit.

An idea dawned. It was a risk. There was a chance it wouldn't work. But the Canadians wouldn't laugh at her today. Not after she'd saved Amy. And even if they did, laughter couldn't hurt her.

"Cut a loaf of bread into small squares," she ordered Minnie as she reached into the wooden box and pulled out the softest block of butter. "And when you're done, hand me the knife."

Minnie opened her mouth to argue, but when she saw the look on Lesia's face, she picked up the knife and started cutting. Within minutes, Lesia had buttered two dozen small squares of bread and laid them on a napkin on her table. When the next person came forward with her hand extended, Lesia told Minnie what to say.

"Thanks are not necessary," Minnie said in English to the middle-aged woman. "But please do try a piece of our bread and butter."

The woman hugged her parcels to her chest and stepped back. She looked over her shoulder like she was waiting for someone. "I don't know."

Lesia sensed her hesitation. "Tell her the bread comes from your mother. That she sells out every time she's here. Tell her the butter is from a new producer," she instructed Minnie. "That it's sweeter and fresher than any that's been sold here before."

Minnie translated.

The woman smiled, shook her head and backed away.

"That is a crazy idea!" Minnie turned on her. "No one in their right mind gives food away. It's—"

"Thank you."

Startled, Minnie broke off. Lesia looked up.

Amy Scott's mother stood in front of them. Her red-rimmed eyes were puffy and her fingers trembled as she twisted a worn handkerchief between them. "Thank you for saving my daughter's life."

Lesia didn't need an interpreter to understand. Nodding, she reached out to take the woman's hands. How awful she must feel to know she hadn't been watching her daughter carefully.

"I . . . I . . . wish there was something I could do . . ." The woman's voice trailed away.

"Tell her I want her to try the bread and butter," Lesia said.

Minnie frowned.

"Tell her!" Lesia insisted.

Minnie did.

Surprised, Mrs. Scott studied her. "That's all?"

"Tell her no one is buying and the butter is the sweetest this side of Brandon. Once people taste it, they will know." When Minnie hesitated a second time, Lesia jabbed her with an elbow. "Tell her!"

Minnie did.

"Ah." The woman smiled. She stuffed the handkerchief in her pocket, leaned over and selected one of the squares with the most butter. Raising it to her lips, she took a bite. Slowly she chewed. Her eyes widened. "That is very good." She reached out, took another square and called over her shoulder. Three people hurried over for their own sample. Soon, there were a dozen people in front of the table. Bread and butter was selling so fast, Lesia and Minnie could barely keep up. Pennies and nickels and dimes lay scattered on the table like flakes of snow.

"Eggs too. She has eggs," someone yelled.

"What's the name of your farm?" a young mother asked. "So we can look for it next time."

Minnie translated.

The name of her farm? It wasn't a farm. It couldn't have a name. Farms were for the Master Stryks of the world. The people who counted.

"Give it a name," Minnie hissed. "It has to have a name so they'll think of it again."

A name. *A farm?* Farms were when you belonged in a place. When it was home.

They were all staring at her. Pairs and pairs of eyes. Canadian eyes. Staring and waiting. Only this time there wasn't judgment in the eyes, nor was there anger or disgust or even derision. There was curiosity. Eagerness. And in one or two pairs of eyes there was the dim light of acceptance.

Had it always been there and she hadn't noticed? Or had her good deed put it there? It was there; that was all that mattered. "Faithland," she said shyly.

Several people nodded, but those in the back of the crowd looked uncertain. "What was that?" someone yelled.

"Faithland Farms," Lesia said with a grin. This time her voice was strong and clear. "We're Faithland Farms. That's who we are."

Chapter Twenty-One

"A farm?" Andrew looked impressed. He pulled on the reins to slow the wagon; they were almost home.

Lesia felt her face flush. "They were all staring at me. I had to say something!"

He laughed, and, after a minute, Lesia joined in. They were both in happy, hopeful moods—Lesia because she had sold out at yesterday's market, and Andrew because Paul had just been released, thanks to a powerful friend who had spoken up on his behalf.

"You realize what today is, don't you?" he asked.

"No, what?"

"It was a year ago today you saw your land for the first time."

With a slight shock, Lesia realized Andrew was right. Today

was May 10. "A lot can happen in a year," she said softly.

"Like having a farm," Andrew teased. "And a fence." He pointed up ahead to where Lesia's fence was just coming into sight. "You'll need a sign now. All good farms have them."

"It's not *really* a farm. It's keeping Faith and the chickens happy, that's all it is."

Andrew ignored her. "And you'll have to have a place to keep all your money," he continued. "Somewhere safe."

She giggled. "My sock works just fine, thank you very much."

"Oh, really?" He reached over his shoulder. "I thought this would be better."

Lesia stared at the square brown package he'd put on the seat between them. Now what?

"Open it."

She couldn't. "I can't take any more gifts." Faith was the final straw. Even Mama agreed.

"It's not a gift," Andrew said. "Now open it before I stop this wagon and open it myself."

One look at his face told her he was serious. She picked up the parcel. It was surprisingly heavy. She ran her hands over the top of the paper. She could feel the raised surface, the familiar outline. It couldn't be! Shocked, she looked up. Andrew was whistling!

"Is it . . . ?" The words stuck in her throat. "How did you . . . ?"

He stopped whistling. "Would you just close your mouth and open the parcel?" he ordered gruffly. But when he glanced at her, his face was indulgent, and his blue eyes were warm with the kind of tenderness she'd seen only once—when he'd talked about his wife.

Hands shaking, Lesia struggled with the thin, green twine. With each twist, her heart raced faster. Then it was off and she was tearing at the brown paper, removing Geedo's beloved Bible and Baba's precious box. Fat, salty tears streamed down her face and plopped onto the wood. "I can't believe you did this," she blubbered. "You didn't have to . . . I can't accept this . . . it's too much . . . another gift." She was laughing and crying, making no sense at all.

"Keep them dry, for heaven's sake." Andrew handed her a handkerchief along with his usual look of amused exasperation.

She wiped her face, blew her nose and then ran her hands over the box: the delicate stems and many-petalled flowers, the tiny bee nestled at the centre of one of the blooms. She opened the Bible and inspected the pages, touching the familiar words with gratitude, checking that Geedo's documentation of his family still remained on the first page. His family. Baba's family. Her family too. It was all there. Both the box and the Bible were untouched. Bozhe! And she had thought she'd never see them again.

"You're always giving me things," she said when she finally trusted herself to speak.

"I'm not giving you anything." Andrew turned onto the path to their homestead. "I'm returning something that belongs to you. There's a difference."

"But you had to pay to get them back."

"Especially for the box," Andrew chuckled. "That old man drives a real hard bargain."

"I'll pay you back. Out of my market money."

"I won't take it."

"I don't like debt. I guess I'm my father's daughter, after

all." She smiled at the irony. "How much were they, Andrew?"

He was silent a long time. Finally he turned to her and said, "Some things are priceless. To put the value of a dollar on those would cheapen them."

"But you—"

"No." He pulled the oxen to a standstill. "Both the Bible and the box have been passed down through your family, from mother to daughter and father to son. They are a part of your heritage, Lesia. You cannot give that up."

"But it wasn't up to you to recover them for me."

He shrugged. "I can do it, so why not?"

She opened her mouth to argue, but Sonia came tearing into the clearing. "Lessie, Lessie, come quick!" She ran back the way she came towards the garden.

Fearing the worst, Lesia jumped from the wagon and ran after her.

Mama was there, with Adam in her arms and Sonia at her feet. Above her was the bee skep Lesia had woven so many months ago. The one that had been damaged in the wind, the one Mama had insisted on mending. And just below it was a sight Lesia had been praying for.

"Bees!" She stared at the hovering, buzzing mass in awe.

Let your effort be true, my darling child, and your rewards will be sweet.

Tears pricked her eyelids. A lump welled up in her throat. She hugged her precious family Bible close. "We have bees!"

"Just in time," Mama said with a smile, "to welcome you home."

Chapter Twenty-Two

January 2003

Winnipeg, Manitoba

What happened next, you ask?

Ach, my darling Laisha, so much. But so little that would fill a history book.

Andrew, your pra-geedo, was a special man. He asked me to marry him not long after, but I could not while the war was on.

There were still Canadians who disliked us, who still used words like bohunk *and* honky.

There are still those who do it today. You think I do not hear. I do. But I accept. Because accepting brings me peace.

I bought more chickens and another cow. Not as good as Faith, that new one, but she was ours and we loved her.

Ivan and my father were set free. Before the war ended, just like Paul had said might happen. Lots of men were. But they could not come home. No. Instead, they were shipped out like slaves to companies that worked them like horses. We could not see them for two long years.

But Ivan and Papa were two of the lucky ones. Other men were kept in for longer. And they lost everything. Their land. Their money. Their will.

We held on. Papa was never quite the same after. He trusted no one. Ivan was different too. He did not take risks after that. And I never heard him laugh again. Not even when he married and had a son. He turned serious, Ivan did. Though he married a woman who laughed enough for both of them.

Mama never gave up her dream of a real wooden house. And when Papa and Ivan and Andrew built her one, she told me that now she had a palace and she could live like a real Tsarivna.

I still dreamed about Shuparka and, of course, about Baba, but less and less.

Canada became my home.

When Pearl and Paul moved to town, we took over their land. It made sense. It was right beside Andrew's. Paul became a man of decisions. What do you call them? A politician. Imagine, they said. A Ukrainian-Canadian making decisions. And Faithland Farms had the best cream and the best butter and the best eggs. We grew very, very big.

But that was very many years later.

Mama died with a smile. That was the year Andrew and I helped them sell their wheat and they earned enough money to send both Sonia and Adam to school. Papa died two years later. He smiled at the end too. But his smile was for Mama. He was going to find her.

Andrew and I did well together. He gave me many years of laughter, and five glorious children. Your baba was my first daughter. The peaceful one, I liked to call her. Unlike her brothers.

Ach, my darling Laisha, these then are your roots. Yes, it is true. You are Canadian. And yes, you are also Ukrainian.

And you can be both. Proudly.

Shuparka birthed me once, but the prairie birthed me again. All that I am, all that I became, I owe to her. It made me and formed me, just as I formed it.

I am more than Canadian. I am more than Ukrainian. Those are my roots, yes, but I am more than roots. I carry within me memories, and now I scatter these memory seeds upon you.

I give them to you with this Bible and this box. Hold them. Treasure them. If you keep them and share them forward, they are all you will need to live a long and happy life.

Ach, people will tell you, the Bible and the box they are not worth money. But they have been passed from loving hand to loving hand, and, as your pra-geedo told me those many years ago, they are a priceless part of your heritage.

So are the memories. They cannot be found in any history book. But they contain the lessons of life, the things the history books don't tell you. The only things worth having.

To live and to laugh. To love God as no other, for He makes everything right. To find fault with no one and to do your best.

This is all that matters.

I have lived and laughed. I have prayed and grieved. I have birthed children and watched them grow. I have stood in the parched, drought-cursed summer and buried two of them.

Through it all I learned. I learned to accept with good grace what God gave me. I learned that the prairie can be a bitter rival but also a blessed friend. And I learned that all dreams count for something. Big dreams or little ones.

It is as Baba promised when I left Shuparka all those years ago. Let your effort be true, and the rewards will be sweet.

Like the bees, you must go from flower to flower, in wind or rain. In sun or snow. You must stay busy. Work hard. And love.

I have known scorn and ridicule and hatred. I have also known love. And let me tell you, my darling Laisha, love is better.

Always.

Author's Note

While this is a work of fiction, some of the events are based on fact. Over 8,000 people, including women and children, were unjustly interned during Canada's first national internment operations of 1914–1920. The vast majority—about 5,000—were Ukrainian. With them were other Eastern Europeans, including Croatians, Serbians, Hungarians, Poles, Turks and Bulgarians. Added to the difficulty for many Ukrainians was the fact that they weren't allowed to call themselves Ukrainian. Instead they were either called Austrian or were known by various regional names, including Galician, Bukovynian, Rusyn or Ruthenian. Camps and work sites were spread across the country—in places like Banff, Alberta, Brandon, Manitoba, Kapuskasing, Ontario, and Spirit Lake, Quebec. At the same time, over 80,000 other people, the majority also Ukrainian, were forced to register as "enemy aliens" and report regularly to authorities. More than 100 internees died in the camps, and 69 of them were "Austrians." Valuables were also seized during arrests. A report prepared in 1992 by Price Waterhouse estimates that Ukrainian Canadians suffered from $21.6 to $32.5 million in losses while interned.

Acknowledgments

Special thanks to the Ukrainian Cultural and Educational Centre in Winnipeg, especially Larissa Tolchinsky (former librarian) and Zenon Hluszok (former archivist) for sharing time and information; to Sheryl Dunn, Ellen Godfrey, Judith Todd Monroe and Lea Tassie for helpful comments and encouragement early on; to Lois and Larry Peterson for seasonal memories of the prairie landscape; to Jennifer Taylor for her patience and insight; to Orysia Tracz for the depth of her Ukrainian knowledge and her willingness to share; to Dr. Lubomyr Luciuk for his discerning comments on Ukrainian history; to Laisha Rosnau for sharing the story behind her name; and to Julia Eisler for asking just the right question over a bowl of fasolada.